suspense

HAM   Hammond, Gerald.

Pursuit of arms

HAM   Hammond, Gerald

Pursuit of arms

DEC 16   ILL Palenville
MAR 19   Z-6937

GERALD HAMMOND
PURSUIT OF ARMS

48,564

St. Martin's Press
New York

Library of Congress Cataloging in Publication Data

Hammond, Gerald.
  Pursuit of arms.

  I. Title.
PR6058.A55456P8   1986   823'.914   85-25113
ISBN 0-312-65697-1

First published in Great Britain by Macmillan London Ltd.

First U.S. Edition

10 9 8 7 6 5 4 3 2 1

PURSUIT OF ARMS

ONE

The combine harvester with its attendant tractor and trailer turned and began the last cut down the middle of the big barley field. Keith Calder and his brother-in-law waited at the further end. Ideally, they would have liked to walk beside the harvester, but the modern machine moves faster than a man can walk.

Keith recognised the familiar heightening of expectation and knew that it was absurd. When he was young, there would have been a dozen men and more boys, with guns and sticks, waiting for rabbits and rats to bolt as the last of their cover was harvested. But myxomatosis and the changing face of agriculture had taken their toll. There might be nothing to bolt, or just the odd pheasant still out of season. But not to worry. It was a pleasure to wait, in the summer sunshine, courtesy of Neill McLelland the farmer. Lairy Farm lay in a dip so that its closeness to the southern fringe of the town was not apparent. But for the main road traffic, angling up the slope of the hill, they could have been deep in the countryside.

Keith stole a glance at the far corner of the field where Neill McLelland was operating the baler. He was, Keith noted with displeasure, making the huge, round bales favoured by farmers for their easy handling by modern

5

machinery, and not the smaller, rectangular bales which were desired by the pigeon-shooter for hides and by the clay pigeon enthusiasts for protecting the trapper.

The combine harvester was only a hundred yards away now. One hen pheasant, out of range as well as out of season, whirred up from dangerously close to the blades, then set her wings and glided towards the distant hedge. Keith saw the contractor's man, driving the combine, raise an imaginary gun. A hare streaked across the stubble and clapped down into hiding. There would be time to look for it later, but Keith knew that it would not be there. Hares had an astonishing knack for disappearing. No wonder, Keith thought, that they were credited with miraculous powers.

Brutus, the old labrador, nosed his master's leg. But Keith's attention was on his brother-in-law. Ronnie was pointing at the very edge of the barley. 'Fox!' he shouted over the thrum of the approaching machines.

Keith set himself for a shot. No fox would slip by if he could help it. Keith detested foxes, and not only for their predation on gamebirds and domestic fowl. One day, some sentimental fool would smuggle the wrong pet into the country, and with it rabies; and the spread of that shocking disease would depend upon the density of the fox population.

The machines were drowning all other sound. Keith concentrated on watching the edge of the barley.

The fox bolted suddenly on Keith's side. He held his fire for a moment in case the tractor driver should be endangered by a ricochet. The fox could have gone to safety between the tractor's wheels, but it turned away from the lumbering monsters and took a new line past the less obvious menace of the man. Keith kept still, for fear of turning it again. When he judged, from the corner of his eye, that the range was an ideal twenty yards, he turned with practised grace, mounting his gun and slipping off the safety-catch as he turned.

As his forefinger moved to the front trigger, he froze, horrified. A man was approaching him, only a few yards away.

The fox jinked away over the stubble.

Keith raised his barrels. 'You stupid, suicidal moron!' he said. His voice had gone squeaky with fright. 'Didn't your mother ever warn you not to come up behind a man who's ready with a gun?'

'She told me that a man as experienced as you are would look behind him before taking a shot,' the other retorted calmly.

'I looked behind me when I got myself set. I didn't expect some crazy sod to come pussyfooting up behind me. I could have blown your brains out, if you had any. As it is, I'd have filled the air with sawdust and parrot-crap.' Having relieved his feelings with what he felt to be a well-phrased rebuke, Keith took his first calm look at the newcomer; a small, elderly man, grey and wrinkled and with full, fat lips. In the heat of the moment and meeting the other out of context, Keith had thought him a stranger; but now the penny dropped. 'You've spent your life around guns,' he added. 'You ought to have learned sense.'

'There's a lot of things I ought to've done,' the other said. 'More than I care to think about. But at least I'm not the one standing in the way of the tractor.' Keith moved hastily out of the way. 'I wanted to see you on a matter of business. I called at your shop, and your partner said that you were overhauling guns in your workshop at home. So I drove out to your house. Your wife said you'd gone out. When I pushed it, she said to

7

look for you here. Playing hookey?'

Keith had got over his annoyance, but he made up his mind to keep the other on the defensive. Something told him that bargaining time was not far away. Eddie Adoni, third-generation Italian, was a medium-sized arms dealer of mixed reputation who had occasionally used Keith for the overhaul of modern guns or the disposal of antiques.

'I don't do business in guns with men I can't trust around them,' Keith said. Even to himself, he sounded sulky.

Eddie's plump lips twisted in a mirthless smile. 'I'll take my money elsewhere, then,' he said. 'But we're talking about a lot of cash.'

'You're not just trying to palm off a Chasspot rifle as a Von Dreyse needle-gun again?'

'That was an honest mistake. No, I told you I'm spending money.'

'Then I'll listen,' Keith said sadly. His stolen day was lost to him.

'Let's not talk in a field. My car's in the farmyard.'

'Give me two minutes.'

Keith made his excuses to his brother-in-law, who seemed relieved rather than disappointed at the end to their sport. He found Eddie waiting in the driving seat of a year-old Volvo Estate. Keith dropped his cartridge-belt, game-bag and bagged gun onto the back seat and sat in beside Eddie. 'Business must be good,' he said.

'You've got to keep up a front.' Eddie started the car and drove gently onto the tarmac farm road. He parked in the shade of some trees. The car, which had been standing in the sun, began to cool off. 'Mr Calder – Keith – how would you like to quote for a big contract,

8

overhauling a whole lot of Sterling S.M.G.s and nine-mil Brownings? Re-blue when necessary.'

'How many?'

'Nearly three thousand Sterlings and a thousand Brownings. I don't know the exact number yet. Quote me a per-each price.'

'Not on your screaming Nelly,' Keith said. He thought furiously. He had undertaken such contracts before. He had access to space in the town, an overflow workshop held available by an engineering firm, and several retired engineers and gunsmiths were only too happy to pick up the extra money. But why would Eddie come to him? Keith could never undercut the prices that Eddie could have got elsewhere. 'The Sterlings would only be on the market because they're clapped out,' he said, 'and I'll bet half the Brownings are the old Model Nineteen-hundred.'

'They're all Mark Ones,' Eddie said. 'A lot of them are still in waxed wrapping paper.'

'Great! Those'll be wartime manufacture. The ones by John Inglis of Canada are usually all right, but a whole lot of the ones made in Belgium for the Germans were sabotaged to the point of being dangerous. Every one of them will have to be opened, stripped and checked. I'd only consider it on piecework.'

'Give me some sort of bracket, so that I know we're not wasting my time,' Eddie said quickly. He seemed to have been expecting Keith's obduracy.

Keith thought some more. In competition with Birmingham, he would be priced out. There had to be some other reason for Eddie approaching him. He quoted some rates, but kept them high.

Eddie sighed the sigh of a man who has done his best

for a friend, and started his engine. 'You'd leave me less than no margin,' he said. 'Shall I drop you at home or at the shop?'

'Home,' Keith said. 'My car's there.'

The car moved forward and as they crested a slight rise the town of Newton Lauder grew out of the ground to their left. Almost opposite was the group of new, box-like factories where Keith would find his workshop space if the contract came to him, but almost immediately Eddie was threading the car through the streets of the town, between buildings of weathered stone. Keith turned his face aside as they passed the shop. Soon they were out into the country again. While his mind raced ahead, Keith was content to chat desultorily about John Moses Browning, the amazing innovator who had led the field in so many aspects of gun design. Eddie was silent except for the occasional grunt until they left the road again for a byroad and then for the short drive of Briesland House.

'There is just one other thing,' Eddie said as he brought the car to a halt. 'If you don't want the big job, you might care to take on a smaller one.'

Here it came. 'I might,' Keith said.

'You took out a patent a few years ago . . . .'

'I've taken out eleven patents,' Keith said. He thought that he could make a very good guess as to which one interested Eddie Adoni. 'Don't tell me that you're interested in an artificial pigeon decoy which can flap its wings in a treetop? Or a shotgun safety-catch which locks the action?'

'You know bloody well I'm not. Revolvers. You patented an adapted action which brings the cylinder to rest with the hammer between cartridges.'

10

Keith smiled inside himself, but not a hint of it showed. His guess had been good. 'What about it?'

'Could you convert four hundred?'

'In what sort of timescale?'

'No great hurry,' Eddie said. 'February would do.'

'Depends what model. New Style Engineering make the bits for me, and if they've already got the dies in stock it should be no problem.'

'Webley and Scott thirty-eights, Mark Six.'

'No problem at all,' Keith said. 'We did a whole lot for a Caribbean police force.'

'How much?'

Again Keith thought before he spoke, and again he pitched his price high.

'Oh, come *on*,' Eddie said. 'You'd leave me no margin at all. How about selling me a licence to get the conversions done somewhere else?'

Keith shook his head.

'Well,' Eddie said, 'if that's your attitude I'll just have to take my business elsewhere.'

'Try and take that part of your business elsewhere,' Keith said, 'and I'll slap an interdict on you and then sue your pants off. Let me tell you how I see it. Some small country going independent. The President-elect has to equip, or re-equip, his forces, and you've quoted. He's probably getting a grant for the cost, and if he's spending sterling he's about to become an ex-Brit. The grant would be based on the new prices, so he's buying second-hand and either pocketing the balance or using it for good works, as if we cared which. Very sensibly, he's equipping his forces with an S.M.G. and a self-loading pistol which take the same ammunition, thus breaking the habit, prevalent in such places, of sending troops out

11

with the right gun and the wrong ammo, or vice versa.

'But his police force are the boys who will be near him and responsible for his safety. So he's giving them revolvers for reliability. But, either as a prestige gimmick or because he doesn't want them going off when dropped near him, he fancies having them Calderised.'

Eddie Adoni had been staring out of the windscreen, tight-lipped. Now he turned and glared. 'And what's any of that got to do with the price of fish?' he asked.

'Not a lot,' Keith said. 'Just this. At that sort of numbers and timing, there's only one place the guns could be going. So what's to stop me dropping His Coffee-coloured Nibs a line, suggesting that he can buy his guns wherever he likes – from you, for all I care – but that if he wants the revolvers Calderised, I do all the work, at my prices, for him and not you.'

'You sod! I believe you'd do it. Listen,' Eddie said, 'it's a good deal I'm offering you. Play your cards right and you could win yourself a free holiday in the sunshine, instructing the instructors.'

'No, thank you very much,' Keith said. 'Once, when I was very young and innocent, I went to Africa on a deal like that. Within a fortnight there was a coup, and I found myself acting as armourer to a rebel army. What was worse, it turned out to be the losing side and I was lucky to get out with the same number of balls I went in with.'

'All right. So what do you want?'

'A straight deal, signed and sealed, with no room for your usual tricks. Money up-front. And if I do any of the work I do it all. Given that, I can maybe shave the price a wee bit.'

'I should bloody well hope so. How wee?'

'Not that damn wee,' Keith said cheerfully. 'Hang on

12

while I drop my gear inside and get the car out. Then we'll go back to the shop and let Wallace in on the haggling.'

Keith returned to Briesland House later than usual that evening. After a draft contract had been signed and missives exchanged, he had driven fifty miles without ever being more than five miles from the shop, making sure that his usual force of retired specialists was still ready and willing. From the shop, he had phoned off an order for blueing chemicals. And he had visited the industrial estate to reassure himself that the usual workshop space would be available. To this last he was only able to obtain a qualified answer; his was not the only business in line for a rush of work.

Instead of pausing for his usual admiring look at the house, Keith plunged inside, eager to share with Molly the news of that day's business coup. To celebrate the imminence of 'found money', he had paused in his travels to raid the local shops, bringing home several luxurious toys for daughter Deborah and, more for his own pleasure than hers, some confections of silk and lace to adorn his wife.

But Molly was also brimming with news, in which state she was difficult to override. 'You'll never believe what's happened,' she began.

'Probably not,' Keith said. He vanished into the toilet under the stairs.

Molly's voice followed him through the closed door. 'Ronnie was here. He brought Brutus home. He's in his box.'

'Ronnie is?'

'Brutus. He wants to see you.'

'Brutus does?'

13

'Ronnie does.'

Keith emerged. 'Big deal,' he said. 'And talking about big deals -'

'Ronnie had a girlfriend with him,' Molly said.

'Yet another old boot. Is my dinner ready?'

'Dried up and spoiled. Not another old boot this time,' Molly said reluctantly. 'Very . . . svelte. Lean and athletic and looks as if she could tear telephone directories in half. She sounds German or Russian or something.'

'She certainly doesn't sound like Ronnie,' Keith said. 'Could we discuss her over what's left of my dinner, instead of standing in the hall?'

'Ronnie said that she was a dancer. I think she's moved in with him.'

Keith was having difficulty envisaging Molly's rough-hewn brother in the company of a German or Russian dancer, except perhaps a Hamburg stripper. 'You're sure she's a dancer?' he asked.

'That's what Ronnie said. And, come to think of it, he said she was Polish.'

Keith snapped his fingers. 'I know who she is,' he said. He turned and walked into the kitchen.

Molly trotted behind. 'Who?' she asked. 'Who?'

'I'll tell you when I've got my dinner.'

Molly knew when she was beaten. She put out Keith's roast beef. It was still satisfactorily moist but he had opened a beer for himself, just in case.

'Well?' Molly said.

'Delicious.'

'I'll take it away!'

'A tiger couldn't take it away,' Keith said with his mouth full.

'Oh, Keith . . . .'

Keith relented. He emptied his mouth and rinsed it with beer. 'You remember, last January, you and I and Janet and Wal were going to go through to Glasgow for a night out and to see the ballet of *The Taming of the Shrew* at the King's Theatre, and you cried off?'

Molly nodded. 'Old Minnie had flu and I stayed to look after her. Ronnie took my ticket. I couldn't think why. Ballet isn't his scene at all.'

Keith had to empty his mouth again. 'He thought he was going to see *Kiss Me Kate*. He still thinks that he saw it. Same plot, after all. He was half-cut before we set off and he had a bucketful over dinner. In that state, he could follow the story without noticing that there wasn't any dialogue. He was very taken with Katherina in the first half, when she was fighting with her family and taking kicks at the passers-by. He thought she was a lassie of spirit. He called her "skeich and birkie", which is more than he ever said about the old boots. He spent the second half in the bar, so he never saw the shrew after the taming. He came away with his illusions intact.

'The part was danced by a stand-in, because the *prima ballerina* had pulled a hamstring or something in rehearsal, and I can't say I'm surprised. They made an announcement of the change, and there was something about it in the paper. She was a Polish ballerina who defected when the Moscow State Ballet came to Covent Garden. I forget how her name was spelled, but I think it was pronounced "Butchinska".'

'Then it's probably the same girl,' Molly said. 'Ronnie called her Butch. But how on earth would Ronnie get to know a ballerina?'

'When we left the King's, our way back to the car took

15

us past the stage door and this girl was coming out. I wouldn't have known her in flared, scarlet jeans and a fur duffel coat, but Ronnie can get quite perceptive when he's got a drink in. He took off his hat with a flourish –'

'*Ronnie* did?'

'Believe it or not, yes. He told her how much he'd admired her performance. And he grabbed one of our business cards off me and scrawled his name and address on the back, and said to look him up if she was ever in Newton Lauder. So if it's the same girl, she took him at his word.' Feeling that he had said it all, Keith resumed his meal.

Molly's eyes were wide. She felt that the subject was far from exhausted. 'But, Keith, a girl like that . . . I mean, she makes an impression. She only spoke to us for a few minutes, but already Deborah's made up her mind that she wants to be a dancer. She wants lessons for her birthday; and she's upstairs now, practising. I only hope the ceilings can stand it. Keith, what would a girl like that see in Ronnie?'

Keith knew exactly what she meant. Molly's brother was a rough diamond. 'Beats me,' he said. 'Of course, Ronnie was wearing his best tweeds and the hat with the salmon flies. If she's Polish, she wouldn't realise that he talks like a tinky from the back of beyond. Has she really moved in with him?'

'If she hasn't, she's going to. But that cottage . . . .'

'It's a house. Small, but definitely a house. And don't forget that after it was flooded, that time the canal burst its banks, you and Janet saw that the insurance money was spent on doing it up like a stately home, when Ronnie just wanted to let it dry out and buy a pair of Dicksons off me with the money. And I ended up taking a loss on those Dicksons,' Keith added resentfully.

'Point is, she probably thinks he's the Provost of Ednam.'*

If Molly felt obliged to defend her brother, it was only in support of a fellow-member of the great sisterhood. 'He is sort of *macho*,' she suggested.

Keith dropped his fork. 'Would you say that?'

'I . . . I think so. If I'm right about what the word means. Have you ever met anyone who was less effeminate?'

Keith admitted that he had not.

'Ronnie with a ballerina!' Molly said, summing up. 'A Polish ballerina! Wonders will never cease.'

Several days passed before Keith and Molly were able to satisfy their curiosity over Ronnie's new domestic arrangements. The impending work for Eddie Adoni kept Keith busy. As well as the more routine details, he had to earmark alternative accommodation, in case his usual premises were required by their proper owner, and to make standby plans for the transfer of equipment. He could neither neglect the routine gunsmithing side of the firm's business nor the dealing in antique guns, and Wallace, his partner, had to be relieved in the shop from time to time.

He managed to break one of his journeys to call at Ronnie's home late one afternoon. He found his brother-in-law at home but alone. Keith's experienced eye detected signs that a lady more than a cut above Ronnie's usual conquests was in residence. Ronnie explained that Butch was in work with the Scottish Ballet that week and rarely got back to Newton Lauder before the small hours. That much, Keith already knew.

* This expression, still in ironic use, derives from the fact that Ednam, near Kelso, now a village of little consequence, once ranked among the most important burghs in Scotland.

17

Miss Baczwynska was possessed of a souped-up Mini and drove it in a manner which spread terror among the local road users so that her comings and goings were common knowledge.

On Molly's behalf, Keith invited Ronnie to bring Miss Butch to Briesland House for drinks on Sunday morning, with lunch to follow.

The Calders knew that Ronnie, who was up before dawn on most weekdays, was a reluctant riser on the Sabbath, so they were caught unprepared when the crunch of gravel and the beat of a diesel Land Rover announced the premature arrival of their visitors. Molly ripped off her apron and Keith his gardening gloves, and they met in the hall just as the doorbell chimed. Ronnie ushered his partner in with an air of proprietorial pride.

Molly had met Butch before, but Keith had only seen her on stage and for a few minutes in a dark street so that her impact came at him fresh. She had the lithe fitness and the perfect walk of a dancer, and exuded a vitality which Keith, himself a dynamo of nervous energy, found daunting. Her auburn hair was styled short around a face that showed the gauntness of regular dieting. When she smiled, which was often, she showed large but regular teeth except for prominent upper incisors which, taken with her large and soulful eyes, gave her the look of an affectionate squirrel. She was flamboyantly dressed, in black with a scarlet cape, and clung to a capacious bag of soft leather. Keith found himself blinking. He greeted her with the cautious enthusiasm which he would have accorded to some wild animal and she responded in a deep voice, heavily accented.

'My English is not good,' she said carefully, 'but Ronnee is learning me betterer.'

Ronnie nodded encouragement.

18

Keith was wondering what on earth to say next when Deborah came clattering down the stairs. For a small girl, she always seemed to make an inordinate amount of noise. She greeted the ballerina as an old friend.

'Come and see me dance. I've been practising.'

Molly sighed with relief. 'I must go on with the lunch. My family can look after you, Miss . . . Baczwynska? Is that right?'

'You call me Butch.'

'Do I? I mean, can I?' Molly sounded doubtful. For all her fire and fitness, Miss Baczwynska was far from butch.

'Aabody call me that. And yes, wee one, I see you dance. But for the now, you show Ronnee. I wish to blether with your father about business.'

'That's all right, then,' Molly said. 'Drinks in about an hour.'

Molly retired to the kitchen. Deborah dragged Ronnie away, while leaving him in no doubt that he was, in her view, second best. Keith relieved Butch of her cape, led her into his study and gave her a chair. He watched out of the corner of his eye, to see whether the carefully gracious room impressed her, but she seemed impervious to her surroundings. Disappointed, he sat down behind the desk.

'I explain,' Butch said carefully. 'Ronnee gave me your card. It say you deal with guns, old guns.'

'Antiques,' Keith said. 'Yes.'

'Antics, is right. I ask many chiels who deals in these and ilka time your name is said. A big dealer and more honest than most is what is said.'

Keith, who considered himself to be rather more than a hundred per cent honest with only rare and excusable lapses, was nettled. 'You have an antique gun to sell?'

19

'I have muckle antics to sell,' she said.

Although Ronnie's tuition seemed to be producing a not unattractive linguistic cocktail, Keith felt obliged to intervene. 'You should say "many" rather than "muckle".'

'Many is mair than muckle?'

'Same meaning, but –'

'Aha! Is not good English, muckle?'

'Is not . . . it isn't English at all. Muckle is Scots, many is English.'

'So. I have many guns to sell, is betterer? I want you help me.'

She lifted her bag from the floor. It seemed heavy. Delving among the contents, she produced a fat envelope and passed it over. Keith found that it contained between thirty and forty photographs, all professionally taken to a high standard. He turned his swivel chair away, ostensibly to get better light but in fact because he never let a client see his eyes while he was appraising guns.

As he glanced through the photographs he felt a not unfamiliar vacuum in his guts. Each photograph showed at least one gun, several showed pairs and in one instance there was a whole matching set of sporting guns and rifles. Each specimen appeared to be in mint condition and to be guaranteed to make collectors and curators drool.

Some of this must have shown in his posture. She broke in on his thoughts. 'Is valuable,' she said. 'How much you give?'

'First, I'd want to see them,' he said.

'I bring one.' She felt in the bottom of her bag and withdrew a bundle wrapped in tissue paper. 'None is less good than this.'

The bundle balanced itself in his palm. He unwrapped the tissue paper. The miquelet was in perfect condition. From a glance at its photograph he had assumed that it was one of the many Turkish pistols made to the Spanish traditional design, but on close examination of the decoration in the metal sheathing and the gilt barrel he saw that it was eighteenth century Russian. It belonged in a museum.

On the heels of that thought came another. He laid the pistol down gently on his blotter, rotated the swivel chair again and reached into the tall bookcase for an old, leather-bound book. After some fumbling, he found the plate which he had, vaguely, remembered. He compared it with one of the photographs. 'This gun,' he said. 'The flintlock pistol. This or its twin was in the Kropiniev Museum in Warsaw.'

'Is very old book,' she said quickly. 'Not modern. Kropiniev was private museum of Kropiniev family. When Russians come, family take treasures away and hide them. I have papers.'

Keith tapped the pistol with a respectful forefinger. 'You have the provenance – the papers – for this one?'

'I have here. All is OK. But they are in Polish.'

She produced a slim docket of papers, some typed and some in a thin, spiky handwriting, much faded. On one point, she had not deceived him. They were indeed in Polish. As far as Keith was concerned, they could have referred to any subject under the sun. 'We'll have to get them translated,' he said.

'If they say what you want, how much this one?'

Keith picked up the pistol again. He checked that it was unloaded and then tried the mechanism. He studied the engraving under a lens and dropped a bore-light down the barrel. 'I'd value it at between six and seven

21

thousand pounds,' he said at last.

'You have . . . ?' She mimed the pressing of buttons. Keith gave her his calculator. She translated pounds into zloty. 'Is good,' she said. 'I take six and half.'

For a moment, Keith was tempted. The money could be borrowed. And he would have loved to see his partner's face if he had committed them. Wallace James had developed a new expression like that of an outraged sheep, with which he greeted additions to that part of their stock which they both knew (although Keith denied it vigorously) to be Keith's private collection. But no. This would be too much. Besides, there were even more fascinating specimens shown in the photographs.

'Not so fast,' he said. 'Slow down a moment. If all the guns in these photographs are as good as they look, and if their papers are satisfactory, you have a whole lot of money to come. You understand?'

She nodded. 'A wheen of money,' she said, translating his words into a more familiar idiom. 'Is good.'

'Is not bad at all. My firm might buy one or two of the guns, but the sort of total we'd be talking about for the whole collection would be more than we could have lying out for the time it would take to get the best prices. What we'll do is to sell them for you. Usually we take ten per cent, but for this kind of money we'll do it for five. You understand five per cent?'

She nodded and smiled her squirrel's smile. 'One in twenty. Is fair.'

'Isn't it just!' Keith suspected that her pleasure was in being left a margin for her own commission. 'I send out a catalogue – a list – to museums and collectors, and to other dealers. I'm preparing one now. As soon as I've seen the guns and their papers I'll include them and send the list out. It'll cause a stir.'

She nodded again. 'I get papers – translated, is right word? Guns come in wee ship, will be here soon.'

'I'll want translations certified,' Keith said. 'The Polish Embassy would do it.'

'No embassy. I go to language department of university. Is OK?'

'Is OK,' Keith said. Like Miss Baczwynska, he found idiom infectious.

TWO

Losing his temper with Superintendent Munro had become a habit with Keith Calder, and one which he had almost come to enjoy as the years went by. He was in the process of doing so for perhaps the twentieth time.

'You've got to be out of your tiny Hebridean mind,' Keith said.

Munro, recently promoted from chief inspector on the retirement of his predecessor, was still too gratified to take more than his usual umbrage at Keith. Besides, he had heard it all before. His long face showed a gleam of perverse pleasure. It was his turn to administer the pin-pricks. 'It is no part of my duty,' he said in a careful lilt, 'to give special protection to your goods.'

Keith took several deep breaths and decided to have one more try. 'You,' he said, 'are the one who gets into a knicker-wetting temper on the subject of guns in your territory. And that despite the fact that according to the last review the total of firearms fired during crimes was down. You harass the hell out of anybody who wants a small-bore rifle, although if anyone ever used such a thing to hold up a bank I never heard of it. If you were honest instead of toeing the police policy line, as handed down on tablets of stone by the Committee of Chief

24

Constables, you'd admit that guns mostly reach the criminal via the black market, starting at the back doors of factories and armouries or from looting in transit. And yet, now that I've got a load coming in which would keep organised crime and the I.R.A. tooled up for years, you won't let me use armed guards. Nor will you provide more than a couple of unarmed bobbies to see the load arrive.'

The superintendent settled his bony frame as comfortably as he could in the hard chair. 'Special precautions, in my experience, only draw attention to the fact that there is something worth stealing.'

'Too damn many people know about this load already,' Keith said. 'Whispers have been getting back to me. I've even had an approach from the Manpower Services Commission, wanting to know whether I couldn't employ a few school leavers.'

'But you've no real reason to believe that a crime is being planned?' Munro asked keenly.

'Well, no. I'm just doing my duty to God and the insurance company, and keeping you informed.'

'Don't you fash yourself, Mr Calder,' Munro said comfortably. 'It is true that the nature of your business, and your own character, have attracted trouble from time to time. But nobody steals lorryloads of arms on my patch. We'll keep our eyes and ears open. There'll be a pair of laddies in plain clothes to see the load into your works, and irregular visits from the cars on patrol while it's there.'

'Well, all right,' said Keith. 'If that's the best you can do. But I'm going to write to you, confirming what we've said. Things don't often go agley. But if the day ever comes when I'm in a position to say "I told you so", I want to be able to prove that I said it.'

Butch brought the documents back a week later. Keith followed her into the study. Apart from her dancer's buttocks, which were disappointingly boyish, Keith thought that she had everything. Who was Ronnie, to hit such a jackpot? And did he have enough finesse to appreciate it? Although Keith honestly believed that he had been a model of virtue since his marriage, he was not above coveting his neighbour's goods, especially when the goods were as nicely distributed as Miss Baczwynska's.

She handed over a full set of neatly typed, certified translations. He spent an hour going over them, asking for elucidation of a few points. At last, he pronounced himself satisfied. He had one or two mental reservations, but a collector would not be so hard to please. The customs documents were at least good enough to let Keith plead, in the event of a subsequent enquiry, that he had accepted them in all innocence.

'When do I get to see the guns?' he asked.

'Ship is leaving from Lisbon soon. After that . . . How long until money comes?'

'If you're looking for the cash in a hurry, we might do better to arrange an auction.'

'No unctions,' she said firmly. 'If I wanted unctions, I go to your Crispies.'

'Why not?' Keith asked.

'Because I say. You put guns in your list and send out and we wait for money, is all.'

'In other words,' Keith said, 'the Polish or Russian governments might sit up and take notice if we advertised that a lot of Polish national treasures were drifting into the West?'

'Not for you to worry about.'

'We could stir up a little more interest if we leaked a story to the press,' Keith suggested.

26

'No bloody fear,' she said.

'That's what I thought you'd say.'

An importunate Deborah was waiting in the hall, hoping for an hour or two with her new friend and mentor. While Butch was still trying to escape without hurting the child's feelings, Eddie Adoni arrived. Keith looked upwards in despair. The approach of the grouse season had brought a flood of guns for overhaul or repair and he wanted to get the work out of the way. And the arrival of Eddie suggested that the terms of the final contract were not, after all, agreed.

Eddie looked smaller than ever in the shadow of his companion, whom he introduced as Paul York. Middle-age had taken the edge off York's figure, but Keith put him at six and a half feet tall. He was well proportioned for his height and moved lightly on his feet. Keith found that he was shaking a hand that felt like a paving slab, but the grip was very gentle. He took them into the study which was still faintly charged with Butch's modest perfume.

'The guns will reach you tomorrow week,' Eddie said. 'Are you all set?'

Keith made a note. 'I haven't had final confirmation of the workshop,' he said. 'But I've got an alternative lined up. The men are standing by. I've arranged for a watchman, nights and weekends, but you're remembering that I'm leaving insurance in your hands?'

'That's in the contract.'

'Which you haven't signed yet.'

'All in good time.' Eddie glanced at Paul York. 'Mr York will be looking after my interests while the guns are with you.'

'Their security, do you mean?' Keith asked.

'He can help with that. Mainly, he'll be there to check

the number of jobs done.'

'I didn't know you were putting in a minder,' Keith said.

'You think I'm daft? I'm paying you so much per job, as in your breakdown, and by time for anything not covered. You could be robbing me blind.'

'I could, but I wouldn't,' Keith said.

Eddie's plump lips creased in a smirk. 'Not now, you wouldn't,' he said.

'Does Mr York know anything about gunsmith work?'

Paul York spoke for the first time. 'Enough,' he said. His voice was tenor. Keith had expected something deeper from so large a frame.

'We've been going over your costings,' Eddie said. From inside his jacket he produced a Browning Hi-Power self-loading pistol (commonly called an 'automatic'). 'You put in fifty-five seconds for stripping one of these. Paul did it in thirty-three.'

'You couldn't expect a man to keep up that sort of speed all day,' Keith protested.

'Maybe. But Paul isn't a practised gunsmith. I reckon half a minute's long enough.'

'Rubbish!' Keith said hotly. '*I* couldn't do it in that time.'

'I bet you could. Keith, a six-year-old could do it.'

'Never,' Keith said. 'No way. Impossible.'

'Where's that daughter of yours?'

Keith realised that he had been trapped. Deborah, very much her daddy's girl, had been following him around for years, in and out of his workshop, and taking a lively interest in whatever he was doing. 'She's gone out,' he said.

Eddie raised his eyebrows. There came the sound of a troop of elephants descending the stairs, singing shrilly

28

and off key. 'Is that your wife?' Eddie asked. 'You might just ask her to come in for a moment.'

No summons was needed. The door crashed open and Deborah advanced to Keith's desk. 'Daddy, Butch says I'm making *great* strides.'

'Dancers aren't supposed to make great strides,' Keith said quellingly. 'And you know you're not allowed to come barging in here while I've got visitors. Now, say you're sorry and run along.' He found it very difficult to be severe with this engaging little person, who was beginning to take on the look of his dark and pretty wife.

Although Deborah forgot such rebukes within the hour, she took them very much to heart at the time. 'I'm sorry,' she wailed. Her eyes filled with tears and she backed towards the door.

'Never mind,' Eddie said. He produced his most engaging smile, which nearly caused Deborah to bolt from the room. 'Come here and show your daddy how clever you are. Take this apart, and if you do it quickly I'll give you a pound towards a new dolly.'

Deborah looked at him with something like contempt. She had never cared for dolls. 'If I do it quickly,' she said, 'never mind about the pound, can I keep this?' She picked up the Browning.

Eddie laughed fatly. 'I'm afraid little girls aren't allowed to own such things,' he said. 'But if you do it quickly, I'll give you one of your very own as soon as you're old enough and have your own firearms certificate.'

'You don't know how, do you?' Keith put in.

'Oh, Daddy, don't be silly,' Deborah said, removing the magazine. She pulled the slide back, using all her strength, and caught it with the safety-catch, turned and withdrew the slide stop and disengaged the slide. She

29

compressed the spring to release the nose of the barrel and withdrew the spring and its guide. She removed the barrel and laid it on the desk. 'Is that enough?'

'Quite enough,' Eddie said. He looked at his watch. 'Twenty-two seconds. Very good indeed.'

'Whose side are you on, anyway?' Keith asked Deborah's departing back. 'And who,' he asked Eddie, 'told you that my daughter could strip a Browning?'

'Your partner,' Eddie said. He was grinning.

Keith felt better. If he had to shave the price, Wallace could take the blame. 'You think you'll never have to cough up,' he said, 'but you're wrong. That little madam will want her own certificate the moment she's old enough, and she won't forget your promise. So, before we talk any more, let's have it in writing that you owe her a nine-mil Browning in good working order.'

THREE

There came a bright, clear day, one of those glorious days which, although rare, symbolised summer in Keith's mind. It was a day for getting out with a dog and a gun, reducing the rabbits, decoying for pigeon or controlling predators around the release pens. The coo-cooing of wood-pigeon in the sycamores was, for Keith, a call to arms.

But work was pressing. Guns which had been forgotten since February were still coming in for overhaul. And Eddie Adoni's firearms were on the way.

Eddie's lorry was not due until nearly noon. Keith turned his mind away from the sights and sounds and smells of the great outdoors and settled to work at his bench, upstairs in Briesland House among the racks of antique guns. He took up an ancient Jeffries sidelock and gauged the barrels as he had done at this season for the past fifteen years. It would break Mr Darnleigh's heart, but this time he would have to be told that the barrels were beyond redemption. It was time for sleeving, or for an honoured retirement over the mantelpiece. He laid it aside and took up an A.Y.A.

The phone rang shortly after eleven. Keith waited, in the hope that Molly would answer it downstairs, and

31

then picked up the extension.

'Mr Calder?' said a voice.

'Speaking.'

'I'm driving Mr Adoni's lorry. I'm phoning from Carfraemill. Mr Adoni's instructions weren't clear. Could you tell me how to get to where I'm supposed to deliver?'

'I sent Mr York detailed directions and a map,' Keith said.

'I didn't see Mr York, I saw Mr Adoni himself. He said something about a change of place.'

Keith frowned. It was against his instinct to pass out such information over the phone. 'What make of vehicle are you driving?'

'A DAF,' the voice said, after a long pause.

'You don't seem very sure.'

'I'm not driving my own cab. Couldn't remember, for a moment.'

'Colour?'

'Dark red.'

'I'll wait for you at the first junction to the main road,' Keith said. He disconnected.

With his hand on the phone, Keith took time for thought. The driver would take half an hour from Carfraemill. If that was where he was. And if that really was the driver. He lifted the receiver again and dialled from memory the number of the police in Newton Lauder. The ringing tone sounded only once before the call was answered. He recognised the voice.

'Sergeant Ritchie?'

'Is that you, Mr Calder?'

'It is,' Keith said. 'Is Mr Munro there?'

'Och, no. He's away out in his car.'

'You know about the lorryload of guns I'm expecting?'

32

'I do that,' Ritchie said placidly.

'Somebody just phoned me up, saying that he was the driver and wanting directions. But I gave the owner's leg-man a map and a detailed route to pass on to the driver. And the voice didn't sound right. So instead of telling him where to go, I said that I'd meet him at the north junction.'

Ritchie was known in the town as a calm, unambitious officer; but, as Keith knew, he was capable of quick and logical thought within his own limits. 'I'll send a car to meet you at the junction,' he said.

Keith shot a look out of the window. His car was still outside. 'I'm going to the workshop first,' he said, 'in case the real driver's got there ahead of time. Tell your car to watch for anyone who seems to be watching for me. And it might be wise to have a car at the other junction as well.' Newton Lauder was unusual in that only two junctions to the main road gave access to the town and its hinterland.

'If there's a car to spare,' Ritchie said doubtfully. 'One's already at your workshop. 'You'll not suggest I move it?'

'No, by God! Do what you can, and let the superintendent know. It's likely that I'm getting in a panic over nothing at all. But all the same . . . .'

'Aye,' Ritchie said. 'Just as well to mak' siccar.'

Keith knew that his most sensible course would have been to remain at home and near the telephone. But the more he thought about that phone-call, the less he liked it. And it would have run contrary to his impatient nature to have stood by and put his trust in the power and intelligence of a couple of unarmed policemen while there was likelihood of an attempt being made on anything that belonged to him, or was his responsibility, or indeed anything in which he had even the most fleeting interest. He ran downstairs and called to Molly that he was going out.

Molly popped her head out of the kitchen. 'Take Deborah with you. She's playing in the car.'

'I wish you wouldn't let her do that,' Keith said. 'She fiddles with everything.' But it was quicker to accede. He darted out to the car. Deborah saw him coming. She scrambled over into the back seat and strapped herself in. Her expression dared him to try to evict her, on penalty of a screaming tantrum. Keith only sighed. He started the engine, switched off the lights, radio, wipers, heater and demister, pushed the seat back and rammed the car into gear.

'Go *fast*, Dad,' Deborah's voice commanded.

'Just for once, Toots, I'll oblige you.' He urged the car out of the gates and fastened his own seat-belt as they wallowed too fast along the uneven byroad. Then they were out into the road to Newton Lauder, once the main road between Edinburgh and the south but now by-passed. He used the gears to coax maximum acceleration out of the hatchback and was doing eighty before they overtook a lumbering artic. in the teeth of an oncoming car. Deborah was singing, always her sign of great joy. He held his speed for a few more seconds and then the streets of the town were ahead. He would have forced his way through at speed except that nothing must distract the police from their set course. So he cruised through the cluttered streets at forty-odd.

The streets were thinning as they neared the southern outskirts of the town and Keith pulled the car hard left into a young industrial estate. The gaily coloured box-like structures lacked the dignity of their stone-and-slate precursors, but Keith had had to admit their many advantages. The first units were all let and the area showed sign of life, if only in the number of vehicles occupying the neat bays. Further in, beyond a tract of unbuildable land where landscaping had already been prepared and planted, the buildings began again, but of the six so far constructed, only the one that Keith had rented was so far in any sort of occupation.

The six units were built around a small courtyard. Keith stopped at the gateway and wound down his window. Two men in suits stepped out from behind the screen wall where, Keith thought, they had been enjoying a quiet smoke. Keith recognised both of them. The older, a sallow man with narrow eyes, had once trapped him with the breathalyser, although Keith had been exonerated by the blood test and the skin of his teeth. The other, a pink-faced youngster, was a very active member of the clay pigeon club. Beside the loading doors, a small knot of men were playing cards on a discarded packing-case. A van was parked beside them.

'No word or sign of the truck?' Keith asked.

'Nothing,' said the older man.

'Be canny. There may be something up.'

The elder nodded. 'We just had word on the radio.'

Keith craned his neck to look at the labourers. There were faces which he could not see.

'Each of them has a letter signed by yourself,' the younger man said. 'I checked.'

'Good!'

The older constable, overcoming his reluctance to admit his ignorance, was ready with questions, but Keith ignored him. He spun the car in the width of the road and lay-by and accelerated towards the street. Rather than go back through the town, he turned left – the driver, even of a vehicle coming from the north, might well prefer to come by the south junction, which had an easier turn for long vehicles.

Clear of the town, the traffic thinned again. Keith built up his speed. He slowed again when a tractor and trailer loaded with straw bales prevented him from overtaking a small car; then up to speed again. Three cars approached; a driver pulled out to overtake but drew in again when he saw Keith's speed and realised that no quarter would be given. Keith slowed again for the right-hand curve towards the main road. The junction was deserted, but as he turned right and began to climb the long hill he saw in his mirror a police Range Rover arrive from the south.

A low-loader passed him, descending in a howl of gears with a small crane on its back and a comet-like tail of impatient cars. Then he had the road to himself. He swung to his right so that he could look down towards the town. No large vehicles seemed to be moving on the lower road. He pulled back to the left and climbed for another half-mile, then crossed again to the wrong side. Now he could see two articulated lorries heading south into the town. One was blue and seemed to be in the livery of the local carrier. The other, grey, looked plain.

At a scream from Deborah and a blare of sound he looked forward again. Siren blasting, another mammoth of the road was bearing down on him, already huge against the sky.

It was too late to brake. Keith stamped on his accelerator and spun the wheel, hoping against hope that no other vehicle was overtaking. He went clear with nothing to spare. The car rocked in the wind as a blue wall rushed by. He twisted the wheel back but his momentum was too great. The nose dipped, the car understeered and he thumped into the banking and stalled. The monster rushed on down the hill, its siren blaring contempt. Keith wondered whether this was the vehicle which he had been trying to intercept. He twisted his head round. He found that he could still see the junction, but the blue shape held straight on.

Shaking, Keith restarted his engine and backed out into the carriageway. Deborah had whimpered but was now quiet. He threw her a reassuring word. The bodywork damage seemed slight, but as he pulled away he found that the steering was unsteady even at modest speeds and at over fifty a serious wobble set in. He curbed his impatience and held his speed down to forty-five for the mile or two remaining.

At the north junction, a single police-car was halted, its occupants boredly watching the empty road. Keith stopped, window-to-window with the driver.

'Anything?'

The driver recognised Keith and shook his head. 'Nobody showing any interest.'

'Have any heavy vehicles turned in since you've been here?'

'None at all. But we crossed with two on the way out.'

'I saw them from the main road,' Keith said. 'Was the blue one local?'

The driver shrugged, but the other man leaned across. 'It belonged to some firm in Greenock,' he said. 'I noticed because I've family there.'

'The load was coming from Clydeside,' Keith said, 'so

that was probably it. And if he didn't wait here, the phone-call I got was a fake. They told you about that? It was a trick and I think I've fallen for it. I suggest you get on your blower and tell Sergeant Ritchie what I said. If he's wise, he'll send more men to the factory. I'm going back there now.' As he drove off, he saw the police driver already speaking into his microphone.

It is human instinct to set off along the route which points most directly at the destination. Keith took the old, low road for Newton Lauder. 'Keep your eyes peeled, Toots,' he threw over his shoulder. 'We may want to remember what cars we've seen.' He had a momentary qualm that the other road would have been faster and would have given him again his bird's-eye view of the town, but by the time they passed Briesland House the vibration in the steering had reminded him that his speed was limited; the shortest route was the best. He called again on his slight reserve of patience and reminded himself that he had no real cause for alarm. So Paul York had forgotten to pass the route to the driver. Or the driver had lost it and was trying to hide the fact. And the voice on the phone had not been English trying to sound Scots, but Scots trying to sound less regional. And perhaps the man really had forgotten what make of cab he was driving . . . He fought off the urge to clear his way with his horn, and threaded decorously through the town.

As he neared the centre he was warned by the sound of klaxons and slowed to a crawl. In succession, three police cars slewed through the square and headed south. The traffic opened for them. Keith fell in behind. This might be no more than a response to his message. But no, there was an ambulance in his mirror. Ahead of him, two cars headed into the industrial estate while the third took up

38

position at the entrance.

Keith stopped and reversed into a side street and let the ambulance go by. In the certain knowledge that the worst had happened, he knew that Deborah must not go there with him. He turned the car back towards the square, to leave her with Janet at the shop.

FOUR

The sunshine was grey and irrelevant, and the front of Briesland House had lost its power to solace. The bright flowers might have been blown toffee-papers. Keith sat still in the driver's seat and gripped the wheel until Molly thought that it would break. 'God!' he said. 'It was terrible. Just terrible.'

'But what *happened*?' Molly asked again. Hearing the car but waiting in vain for her family's boisterous entry, she had gone out to find Keith sitting alone in the car and staring sightlessly through the windscreen. She had sat down beside him, ready to give comfort, but Keith had been less than coherent.

'Bloody awful!' he said, not for the first time.

Molly tried a fresh approach. 'You guessed that there was something wrong,' she said. 'You phoned the police. You went to the factory and everything seemed to be all right. You drove out by the south junction and up the main road, putting a bash in the car on the way. Right so far?'

Keith pulled his mind back from the pit. 'Right,' he said.

'You spoke to the police at the north junction and then drove through Newton Lauder again, and you turned back to drop Deborah with Janet at the flat?'

'At the shop,' Keith said. 'Wal was out.'

'That was sensible,' Molly said briskly. 'I knew she was there, because I phoned up to find out what had happened to the two of you. And I knew something bad had happened because Janet told me the state you were in and she said that police-cars had been rushing around. Now, when you got to the factory, who was there . . .? Was Mr Munro there?'

Keith seemed to shake himself awake. 'He was there. He'd arrived while I was dropping Deborah. There were two police-car crews and the ambulancemen and one of the men I'd hired to do the unloading. He'd turned up late. That's how he was alive.'

'The others were dead? *All* of them?'

'I don't know.' Keith dropped his voice to a whisper. 'The driver of the lorry. Four policemen – Ritchie had sent out two extra on my say-so. And three of the labourers I'd hired. That's . . . seven?'

'Eight,' Molly said.

'Oh, dear God! And I'm to blame!'

Molly had still not caught up with all the facts, but one thing she knew for sure – nothing was ever Keith's fault. 'Don't you go thinking those sort of thoughts. I'm sure it was nothing of the sort.'

'If I'd been quicker off the mark – '

Molly dragged one of his hands off the wheel and gripped it tightly, for her own comfort. 'Then you'd probably have been killed too,' she said.

'But if I'd gone round the circuit the other way, I could have diverted the lorry or something. I don't know what.'

'No, you don't,' Molly pointed out firmly. 'You're only guessing. Was it very terrible?' She had decided that it

41

would be better for Keith to talk it out now.

Keith gave a shuddering sigh. 'I never saw up close,' he said. 'They kept me hanging around in the car while they thought of more and more questions. There was nothing to be seen. No lorry, of course. But I . . . I saw them taken to the ambulances, and none of them were walking. I think one or two must have been alive, because I could see that they were being given oxygen, but at least one or two had their heads covered. I couldn't tell which was which at that distance, but somewhere among them would have been Willie Adams. I hired him to help unload. He is – or was – unemployed. I thought I was doing him a favour. Then that chap McNaught came out, the prematurely bald one – '

'The man who buys the tackle for the Police Angling Club?'

'That's him. He went behind the wall for a puke and came back looking green. He didn't seem to be in any hurry to return. He said it looked as if they'd been made to sit down in a row and then been clubbed. He was going to tell me something else, but he had another attack of the heaves and by the time it was over Munro was asking me more questions. Munro was all grim and uptight and wouldn't tell me anything.' Keith choked.

'And all for the sake of a few guns.'

'Not exactly a few . . . .' Keith suddenly slammed his fist against the steering-wheel and swore again. 'I've just remembered. Butch's guns were on that lorry.'

'Oh, dear!' Molly said as mildly as she could. 'How did that happen?'

'Eddie's guns were coming from his warehouse in Gourock. Butch's antiques came off a ship which docked in Port Glasgow. It seemed a sensible arrangement. I asked Eddie and he didn't mind.'

42

'Does Butch know they've gone?'

'I don't suppose so, in the circumstances,' Keith said. He put his head down again. 'Oh, dear God . . . !'

As Superintendent Munro had suggested, because of Keith's nature and of his professional activities he was a natural attracter of trouble to himself and those around him, so that Molly had had more than normal experience of treating those suffering from physical or psychological shock. Her methods were her own. She hauled Keith inside and forced a large measure of whisky into him, followed by some hot food. Then she drove him, still protesting, upstairs and into a long, hot bath, and thence to his bed. She left him to his fretting while she used the telephone to arrange for the return of Deborah from the shop and the collection of the car for repair. Then, when she judged that the whisky had passed far enough through his system for safety, she fed him three tablets which had been prescribed for herself on an occasion when one of Keith's exploits had brought her to the brink of a breakdown.

Keith, half doped and more than a little drunk, felt far from sleepy. But he knew that Molly was right. He stretched and relaxed and then forced his mind to ignore the disasters of the day and to dally with more soporific subjects. He slept, restlessly at first. But when Molly came to bed she teased him into wakefulness and they made love. Afterwards, he dropped into deep and healing sleep.

In the morning Molly left him, still dozing, and it was nearly midday before he joined her downstairs, shaved but still dressing-gowned, wan but in control of himself again. 'What did you hit me with last night?' he asked.

'Enough,' Molly said.

'Enough is right. Yesterday . . . it wasn't all just a bad dream?'

'I'm afraid not.'

'What's been happening?'

'I only know what's been said on the radio, which is no more than you told me. Could you manage some breakfast?'

'I think I could.' Keith sounded surprised. 'Something to tempt a delicate appetite.'

'Tea, scrambled eggs and toast?'

'That sounds suitably invalidish. Is Munro still in charge of the case, do you know?'

'The radio said something about the Serious Crimes Squad being called in.'

Keith dropped into one of the Windsor chairs. 'I was hoping he'd be too busy to come pestering me,' he said. 'But if they've put somebody else in, he'll have nothing better to do than subject me to one of his tongue-lashings. And for once, he'll have a wee bit of cause. Well, it'll make a change for him, but I could have done without it just now. I'm not ready to face people yet. Has Wal been after me?'

'I phoned to say that you were taking the day off, to get over things. There isn't anything urgent. An order came in the post for one of the tap-action flintlock pistols in the catalogue, but I said I'd deal with it. So you just relax. Do some gardening.'

'Does Butch know yet that her antiques have gone adrift?'

'I told Ronnie to tell her.' As Molly spoke, the doorbell rang.

'In that case,' Keith said, 'that's probably her, come to scratch my eyes out.'

'I think she's in Edinburgh,' Molly said. 'I'll go. If it's

44

for you, shall I send them away?'

Keith thought about it. 'Not if it seems important,' he said. 'I don't feel like going out to face the world yet. Stupid though it is, I'd have the feeling that people were pointing me out behind my back as the man who made yesterday's cock-up. But if the world comes to me, I'll see it.'

'Well, all right,' Molly said as the bell rang again.

Keith braced himself for the impact of the world from outside. He hoped that the visitor was a canvasser, a salesman, a customer, but he knew that on this day of all days it was too much to hope for. As long as it wasn't Munro . . . .

It was Munro, neat as always in his uniform but with a look of angry exhaustion about him. Keith nodded to the chair opposite. The superintendent folded his lean frame and sat down with a sigh.

There was a silence. Neither man felt ready to speak.

Despite the tensions which seemed to clog the very air, or perhaps because of them, Molly became the perfect hostess. She poured another mug of tea.

'Aye,' Munro said. He sounded more Highland than ever. 'I could just be doing with that.'

'Have you eaten? It'd be no trouble . . . .'

Munro waved his hand vaguely. 'I could not be eating just now.'

'You've been up all night?' she asked.

'Not quite that. At four this morning I was put off the case, displaced by the Serious Crimes Squad. I managed a while in my bed. Then I was up again and visiting a widow. It seemed to be the one thing for me to do.'

Silence fell again.

'It's you, then,' was all that Keith could find to say.

The superintendent fixed him with a look which Keith

45

could only feel to be accusing. Just when Keith was about to burst into excuses and apologies, Munro spoke. 'Say it, then.'

'I beg your pardon?'

'Don't shilly-shally, man,' Munro said irritably. 'Say it.'

'Say what?'

Munro sighed. 'You are the *duine uasal* who was wanting to be able to say "I told you so". You will never have a better chance to say it. So enjoy yourself. I was wrong, and two men died.'

'Two?' Molly put in. 'Not eight?'

Munro shook his head. 'One of my men had a thin skull. So also had one of the labourers.'

'Willie Adams?'

'No. The young man Campbell with the stripe in his hair. So if you want to remind me of what you said, now would be the time.'

'I'd forgotten saying anything of the sort,' Keith said. 'Put it out of your mind. I've been calling myself every name I could think of. Because if I hadn't gone dashing off round the countryside – '

'You behaved with sense,' Munro said. 'And it was your actions which prevented a worse tragedy. It is time that you were told the rest. You know that the men were clubbed? The plan may have been to leave it at that or to kill them some other way. But the foreman's van was standing there and offered them the chance to make a clean and certain sweep in silence and without leaving any evidence behind. The unconscious men were loaded into the back of the van and a piece of plastic pipe left by the workmen was led from the exhaust to a hole punched in one of the back doors. They left the engine running. Your warning brought our men on the scene in time, but another minute would have been too late.'

'All the same,' Keith said, 'I shouldn't have gone to the factory at all. If I'd gone the other way to meet the lorry, then –'

'If I'd listened to you and posted a larger, armed guard,' Munro said, 'or if I'd stayed in my office to take your message –'

'Hoy!' Molly said. It came out louder than she had intended. The two men, who had quite forgotten that she was in the room, stared at her. She blushed but plunged on. 'I never thought I'd live to see the day when you two would be sitting down, in the face of a disaster, and each wanting to take the blame. Instead of beating your breasts and crying *mea culpa* – are those the right words?' she asked anxiously.

'I think so,' Keith said.

'It's what Ralph Enterkin said when he trod on Brutus. Instead of crying and . . . and trying to exonerate each other, why don't you *do* something?'

'Like what?' Keith asked.

'I don't know. That's for you to decide. You've never been stuck before.'

'There is nothing to be done,' Munro said heavily. 'The whole case is out of my hands. The Serious Crimes Squad has taken over. They have set up an incident room in an adjoining factory and my sole function is to provide them with men and equipment. I am not even being consulted, just asked to make a statement like any ordinary witness. I am already almost a leper. I am the man who failed. And it will be worse if . . .' Munro stopped and rubbed his face. Keith had never seen him so distressed. 'The reason I came here, Mr Calder . . . Keith . . . was to ask whether that letter of yours must come out.'

47

'I don't see how it can be stopped,' Keith said. 'I sent a copy to Eddie Adoni, and he'll have passed it on to his insurers already.'

'That is it, then,' Munro said forlornly. 'I am in bad enough odour as things stand.' He shook his head. 'When my superiors learn that I turned down a written request for extra protection –'

'When the press hears that I've lost half a million quid's worth of a client's guns,' Keith said, 'plus about half as much again for Butch's antiques – '

'You're doing it again,' Molly said. 'It's not like you, Keith, to be so negative.'

'You're the one who's always telling me not to get involved,' Keith pointed out.

Molly sighed in exasperation. 'I'm not trying to encourage you to leap on a white horse and go gallumphing off in all directions, trying to recover the guns single-handed and being a damned nuisance to everybody, which is about your usual style. But the thing you do well, and which comes in useful, is using your local knowledge and what you know about guns and things to puzzle it all out. Surely it's better that you and Mr Munro try to come up with some answers of your own than that you sit here mumping and wait for the axe to fall. Mr Munro, would the man who's in charge now be helpful and sympathetic?'

'Oh, aye,' Munro said. 'Sandy Doig and I started our careers together. We were good friends once. He's a chief superintendent now. He's got further than I have, further than I ever will with this in my record.'

'He's a fair man?'

'He is that. I see what you're getting at, Mistress Calder. I must not take official action in the matter, being off the case. But if, from the facts of the matter or

48

from local knowledge, I could make a contribution to the solution of the case or to the conviction of the culprits, he would certainly give me credit in his report. It would go a long way to wiping the blot off my copybook.'

'It's a tall order,' Keith said. 'What will Doig be doing now?' Molly was pleased to note that he had lifted his head. His face had come part-way to life again. He was becoming interested. She turned away to hide a smile. Keith, in pursuit of whatever game, was a different being from Keith moping.

'He will be going by the book,' Munro said. 'He is a man of routine. Very thorough, but not an original thinker. He will rely on road-blocks, searches, house-to-house enquiries, informants, known offenders, *modus operandi* and forensic evidence.'

'Good enough in their way,' Keith said. 'For all we know, they're turning up the goods at this very moment. But we have to move on the assumption that it may need something a little more tailor-made to turn up a whacking great vehicle which seems to have been magicked out of existence.'

'He has a helicopter search going,' said Munro, 'and a dozen of my men out looking for tyre marks among the forestry.'

'Give me some camouflage netting and three different colours of paint,' Keith said, 'and I'll hide a dozen vehicles in that forestry. There's mile upon mile of it, and some of it's forty years old and been thinned twice. They've been felling on Low Top and Long Brae, and replanting on Yarrow Hill, so the tracks and firebreaks have been criss-crossed by machinery and trailers. And it's been dry as a bone for a month past. I don't hold out much hope of a reallocated beat-copper spotting the signs of an artic. going by.'

49

'Ronnie would, though,' said Molly.

'That's true,' Keith said. 'And, as Sir Peter's stalker, he can wander around up there without anyone paying attention to him.'

'Keith knows the countryside,' Molly said, 'and the gun trade and the local people. And you know, or can find out, what Chief Superintendent Doig and the rest of the police are doing or not doing.'

Munro still looked like a moody camel, but that, Keith knew, was his natural expression. The deep gloom which had surrounded him on his arrival had lifted. He was almost smiling. 'I can't deny,' he said, 'that you have beaten the police . . . beaten *me* to the punch before now. By the Lord, it's worth a try!'

'Come through into the study,' Keith said. 'We'll set up our own incident room and use the telephone to get things rolling.'

Alone at last in the kitchen, Molly sighed with relief. Now she was free to get on.

FIVE

The phone-call from Paul York interrupted Keith and the superintendent while they were marking a large-scale map with routes which the lorry could and could not have taken, preparatory to calling on Molly's brother. Keith took the call, covered the mouthpiece and said, 'It's Eddie Adoni's agent, minder and security man.' He switched on the amplifier so that Munro could hear both sides of the conversation.

'This is a hell of a pickle,' York said.

'It's that and more,' Keith said. 'Where were you? I thought you were going to travel with the goods.'

'I was going to follow them. But Eddie kept me talking – mostly about watching out that you didn't put anything over on him – and the lorry set off before I was ready. Then I was hurrying to catch up and I got caught in a speed trap, which cost me more time. I was nearing Newton Lauder at high speed when I heard a news flash about the hijacking, so I turned round and went back to confer with Eddie. He wants me to ask what you're doing about it.'

'What the hell are you getting at, York?' Keith demanded.

'Don't get on your high horse. Eddie's inclined to hint

51

that you know something, but we don't think you're at the back of the hijack. Not your style at all. I wouldn't put it past you to switch guns on Eddie, palm off some older junk on him – if there is such a thing – and then charge him for overhauling it. Maybe giving His Nibs a kickback to sweeten some side-deal. But you've become too much the respectable businessman to get involved in robbery with murder. You'll be taking an interest, if only because of the boxes we were carrying for your friend. You've a reputation for dodging around very fast when the shit's flying. What I want to know is, are you collaborating with the police or are you hunting your own line?'

Keith sensed that he was being led onto dangerous ground, an impression confirmed by Munro's sudden look of concern. He decided to talk much and say little. 'I'm not withholding anything from the police,' he said. 'But as far as they're concerned I'm only the man the guns were in transit to but never reached. I'll certainly be keeping my own ear to the ground. After all, I have a responsibility to the owner of the other boxes.'

'You have a responsibility to Eddie also,' York said sharply.

'I don't see it,' Keith said. 'Eddie was supposed to deliver his guns to me and he didn't do it. I don't mind being helpful.'

'You'd better be as helpful as you can. Eddie can be trouble.'

'Eddie's always trouble,' Keith said. He hoped that, like Munro, Eddie was listening. 'Eddie's as nice to have around as a feral ferret. What do you want from me?'

'I want in with you. Eddie means to have those guns back.'

And, Keith thought, without the police or his insurers

knowing it. 'What had you in mind?' he asked.

'Exchange information. Pool resources. Act in concert. Will you be in this evening, nineish?'

'I expect – '

'See you then.' Paul York disconnected.

Keith hung up and switched off his amplifier. 'It looks as if I may be playing for two different teams,' he said.

'Just as long as you remember which team you want to win,' Munro said.

'I'll remember,' Keith said. He picked up the phone again. There was no answer on Ronnie's number, which was not surprising in the middle of a working day. 'He'll be stalking,' Keith said. 'It's the roe season, and farmers have been complaining again. We'll leave Molly to get a message to him through his boss. Molly can twist Sir Peter round her little finger.'

'Is that wise?' Munro asked.

'It's necessary. He's Ronnie's employer. He also employs all the foresters and a lot of estate workers. You don't suspect Sir Peter Hay?'

Munro shook his head emphatically. 'I do not. But he's a romantic old fool. Give him just one hint that you are embarked on one of your escapades and he will be after you like a shot, wanting to join in what he thinks to be the fun.'

'Probably,' Keith said. 'And a damn good thing too. How much good do you think Doig's house-to-house enquiries will do him?'

Munro sighed and shrugged at the same time. 'About half as much as they should. That's the best we ever do.'

'Exactly. And why? Because half the men you're talking to have memories of being breathalysed or prosecuted for a chimney fire or some other footling thing, or they're wondering whether they've let some

53

licence lapse, or they're reluctant to say anything in case they drop a neighbour in the clag and make bad relations. The very men who might have seen the lorry heading into the hills are the foresters and farm workers who're working all hours at this time of year, and they're just the men to be thoroughly scunnered with you after being buggered about with their firearms and shotgun certificates. But ask them the same questions through Sir Peter, who's very popular with his men, and you may get some answers.'

'Swings and roundabouts,' Munro said. 'But be careful what you say. My name must not come into it. Now, shall I give you a lift into the town? I must go in and arrange for a day or two off.'

'Wouldn't it be more help if you stayed on duty? You'd know all that's going on,' Keith pointed out, 'and have access to all the facilities.'

'If I stay in the office,' Munro said, 'I shall be snowed under with all the trivia of day-to-day police routine; and it would certainly be noticed if I took an interest in the investigation. No, Keith, I can find out all that I need to know through my own men.'

'That sounds reasonable. All right, I'll be glad to have you with me. You call in at your office, arrange for some time off and find out as much as you can about the progress Doig may have made. Then go home and change into plain clothes. You can pick me up near the shop after I've made sure that we're tapped into the other lines of local gossip. And we'll call the team together for a meal this evening. We'll keep you out of sight when Paul York turns up.'

'That would be necessary,' Munro said. 'If he is the man I'm remembering, he's ex-police.'

'I guessed that. And, from the way he moves, a karate

54

man. I think he's got something to tell us. Why isn't he getting all the help he wants from Chief Superintendent Doig? Did York leave the police under a cloud? Tampering with evidence, maybe?'

'Suspicion of that,' Munro said. 'And intimidating witnesses. A rough character altogether. I would not be trusting him.'

'I will not be trusting him either,' Keith said, in conscious imitation.

Superintendent Munro was waiting in his car in the back lane behind the shop when Keith arrived at their rendezvous with a bag slung over his shoulder. He sniffed disapprovingly as Keith got into the car. 'You have been drinking,' he announced.

'If a half-pint of lager counts as drinking,' Keith said, 'I have. I was in the hotel, asking Mrs Enterkin to keep note of any bar gossip. Let's go out by the south junction.'

'If you say so.' Munro coaxed the car along the narrow lane and out into the main street. 'I will be off sick for a few days,' he said. 'For the record, I have a slipped disc; but my men think that it is only my nose that is out of joint. Who else have you spoken to?'

'Sir Peter's going to ask his men what they saw. My brother-in-law is studying tracks at the places we picked on the map. And my partner and his wife are going to chat up the customers in the shop, just in case some angler or bunny-hunter saw a vehicle go by.'

Almost opposite the south junction, a little-used track slanted up the hill. The car climbed until they had an open view of the countryside, the town, and the further hills with their patchwork of plantations and older woodland. Munro parked. The two men quitted the car.

Out of his bag, Keith produced two pairs of binoculars from the shop. While they spoke, they rested their elbows on the car roof and picked over the scenery.

'Sandy Doig would tell me nothing about his progress,' Munro said grumpily. 'He said that he was in a hurry. It may even have been true. But my inspector looks to me for his next step up, so he gave me what you would call the "gen".'

Keith had never used the word but he let it go by. 'What did he say?'

'My lad would not know all that the chief superintendent knows,' Munro said, 'but they do not seem to have got very far. After all, it is barely twenty-four hours since the event. There is no sign of the trailer, but the cab which pulled it has been found. It had been parked during the night, bold as you please, among others in the carrier's yard. It was a Leyland, like the others, and the same colour, and was only noticed when the others went out. Whoever drove it through the town had the devil's own nerve.'

'Who'd be looking for a trailerless cab if he went quickly?' Keith asked rhetorically. 'On the other hand, maybe he waited for dark. Most likely of all, he dropped the trailer off at its hiding-place somewhere towards or inside the forestry and then headed north – there's a rough sort of a road – and only came down to the carrier's yard after dark.'

'There have been no tyre tracks found,' Munro objected.

'There wouldn't be, with the ground baked hard and so much felling going on. We'll have to hope that Ronnie can do better. Does the trailer have a solid body, or is it a flat bed with one of those canvas affairs over it?'

'It was all metal,' Munro said. 'It seems to me, in spite

of all that you say, that it would be the very devil to hide. If it wasn't that we had cars at the junctions, thanks to yourself, I'd be sure that they'd got it out already.'

'Well,' Keith said, 'unless they've chopped it up, they haven't. You know as well as I do that, apart from those two junctions, every road out of Newton Lauder peters out in the hills. There are one or two ways you can get over the moors with a Land Rover, but not heavily laden enough to get that load out in less than about twenty trips. No, it's in front of us, somewhere.'

Through their binoculars, they scanned the hills which climbed beyond the valley from farmland through the patterned forestry to the moors above. The heather was bright on the high ground. It was going to be a good year for grouse.

'I just can not believe it,' Munro said suddenly. 'How, for a start, would they get it up there, and nobody see them?'

'You see that tree-strip to the right of the factories?' Keith asked. They both turned their binoculars in that direction. 'There's an old road runs through the middle of it. There's a link from the back of the factories, which used to serve Oldbury Farm. The newest factories are built on the site of the old farm. The contractors were using those roads, but nobody else ever goes along there.'

'Even so, they'd be exposed when they came out above the trees.'

'From up here,' Keith said, 'yes. Down there, they'd be over the crest.'

'A man walking might be over the crest. I think that the top of the vehicle would be in sight for half a mile. And once up there,' Munro added, 'I don't believe that you could hide such a thing. How would you set about it?'

57

Keith felt that he had already covered the point, and he did not feel inclined to give Munro the benefit of the lecture on disruptive patterning which he usually gave to pigeon-shooting courses. 'They probably painted it to look like a brick shit-house,' he said, 'and hung an "out-of-order" notice on the door. I expect your coppers are peeing against the corner of it whenever all the tea catches up with them.'

Munro had learned to ignore Keith's attempts at humour. 'I find it hard to accept,' he said. 'I suppose that the trailer could not be hidden in the town? Some empty building . . . ?'

'Not a chance,' Keith said. 'When it first seemed possible that the workshop I usually take over mightn't be available, it didn't look as if the new factory would be ready in time. There was a delay on materials or something. So I went looking for premises which I could rent. Believe me, apart from that group of factories, there isn't any vacant space at all.' While he spoke, they had turned their glasses left, to where Newton Lauder straggled up the valley, a spread of low buildings, a few spires and the tower of the Police Building standing guard above the bulk of the old Town Hall. Trees lifted above the slated roofs. It was all cosily familiar, and inconceivable as a scene for murder or a cache for stolen arms.

'There's a helicopter over there,' Keith said suddenly.

Munro turned his binoculars and searched to find the speck above the hills. 'It has R.A.F. markings,' he said at last. 'It will be at work for Sandy Doig.'

'It seems to be working a search pattern,' Keith added.

'Doig has already had cars visiting the farms to take a look in the barns and outbuildings.'

58

'Waste of time,' Keith said. 'Look at Lairy Farm down there, on a line with the factories. That's a fairly typical layout. We're looking at the back of the farmhouse. You can see Mrs McLelland at her kitchen window. To the right of it, those buildings are cattle-courts. From lower down, you can see right through them. Anyway, the space is mostly taken up with concrete stalls. Left of the farmhouse, beyond the stack of straw bales, there's a Dutch barn, almost empty at this time of year. You can see into one side of it. One silo and a drying-shed and that's the lot. They used to have a lot of closed-in outbuildings, but they've been replaced with what you see. Farmers don't store a lot of stuff under cover any more. What else has Doig got?'

Munro put down the binoculars on the car roof and stretched. 'Very, very little,' he said, 'and most of that from the survivors. They have been unusually lucid, all things considered. It seems that six men arrived in a big car, on the heels of the lorry. They were masked and they acted as a well-drilled team. They carried sawn-off shotguns. They always do,' Munro said bitterly. 'I would happily see small-bore rifles removed from the Firearms Act if I could see shotguns put on it.'

'When you get your hands on those guns,' Keith retorted, 'if you ever do, you'll find that most of them had never been legitimately held, and maybe the odd one had been stolen from a cabinet which would have satisfied the Act anyway. What else did he say?'

'It was all over in seconds. Four men herded the eight into the yard and made them sit down. They heard the car and the lorry driving off. Then each of the murderers produced what the victims thought was a piece of lead pipe and clubbed two men. That, of course, was the end of it as far as they were concerned.'

59

Keith tried to keep his mind away from the revulsion, but he failed. 'How can men get like that?' he asked.

'Professionals,' Munro said unemotionally. 'Men with records and who have killed before. They knew that the killings might make the difference between being caught and getting away, or between conviction and acquittal, and would add little or nothing to their sentences. Looked at in that way and without compassion, it has a black logic. There will be a leader who makes up in organising ability for a total lack of human feelings. It is not a new pattern.'

Keith shook his head to dispel the pictures in his mind. 'Something must have been said. Could they detect any accents?'

'Only one man spoke. One witness said that he sounded Scots, probably Glasgow, but that the accent did not sound right.'

'Same as I heard on the phone,' Keith said. 'Is that the lot?'

'That's all that the injured men could tell us. They may know more, but the doctors are not letting them be questioned again today. One man did say that he thought that the car might have been red, but that is not to be relied on. Accident victims, for instance, often remember colours as having been brighter than they really were. As to the rest . . . The cab was smothered in prints, but it is unlikely that any of them will belong to our customers. They took the guns and the pipes away with them, so that Forensic do not have much to work with. They are doing their best with a little dust which may have come from afar on somebody's feet. It could help if they could find the car or a witness.'

'You could suggest that they look for a car on the stolen list, neatly parked in the square or in one of the supermarket carparks.'

'They will not have missed that,' Munro said sadly.

'Also,' Keith said, 'you may be overlooking one valuable witness. Don't forget my travels before the hijack.'

'If you saw anything of significance – '

'All that I saw I've told you. But I was driving, and a driver doesn't usually see much but road. My daughter wasn't so hampered.'

'How old is she now? Five?'

'Nearly seven. And she's not your run-of-the-mill Baby Doll witness. She's very observant. She notices cars. And she's noticing men already, the little madam.'

'That would be expected of any daughter of yours,' Munro said. 'If the raid had been carried out by a team of Amazons, you would be able to give me descriptions down to their bust measurements.'

'True, I hope,' Keith said. 'Now, as I see it, the gang had information about the load of arms consigned to me. But . . . Just a minute.' His binoculars had found a target. He blinked to clear his eyes and touched the focusing wheel. But the box-like shape which had shown through a thin screen of trees was the Portakabin which Sir Peter Hay used as an on-site facility for his foresters. 'But at the last minute they heard that I had been squeezed out of the workshop where I'd usually taken such contracts in the past. What would they do?'

'What would *you* do?'

'Good question.' Keith lowered the binoculars and frowned in thought. 'I wouldn't want to shadow the vehicle, not with Paul York supposed to be on its tail. And I wouldn't want to go around asking questions, in case my face was remembered. The wrong question on the telephone might cause alarm. Better to ring Mr

Calder and impersonate the driver. Well, that didn't quite work, but the idiot Calder drove straight to the factory and told them what they wanted to find out.'

'You weren't to know,' Munro said.

'If I'd had a grain of sense, I'd have led them somewhere else. Anyway, they only had to shift their operation a couple of hundred yards, because I usually got space in one of those older factories at the mouth of the estate. I wonder whether their plan would still have worked if I'd found a place at the other end of the town. Well, no sense in speculating until we've gathered what facts we can. I've asked Mrs Enterkin to keep tabs on the bar gossip; and my partner and his wife are letting it be known, through the shop's customers, that I'm desperate for any titbits I can pick up, implying that I'm hoping for news of strangers asking around so that I needn't blame myself for the word getting out. Something useful may get back to us.'

'Aye, it just might,' Munro said. 'Folk will say in gossip what they won't tell the police.'

'Not everybody has my enlightened attitude,' Keith said. 'I keep reminding myself that every policeman is my friend, despite all evidence to the contrary. For the moment, I suggest that we've said all that's worth saying and stared at damn-all quite enough for one day. Let's make a loop through the countryside, just to get the geography and the present stage of the felling into our heads. Then we'll go and interrogate Deborah.'

They got back into the car, but Munro sat quietly for a moment. 'One thing,' he said. 'Will you be hoping for a reward from Mr Adoni's insurers?'

'If we're successful, maybe.'

Munro attempted an engaging smile. 'With your car off the road, I shall be doing a lot of mileage. Would you

62

share the cost of my petrol?'

'Did you come to me or did I come to you?'

'I came to you,' Munro admitted.

'The chances of us finding out enough to get you off the hook would be about even money,' Keith said. 'The odds against our getting enough to screw a reward out of an insurance company must be in the hundreds to one. Pay your own damn petrol.'

SIX

A quick tour of the countryside to the east of Newton Lauder served to convince the superintendent that only a detailed search by many men over a long period could be sure of finding a camouflaged lorry, if it were there at all. When Munro was depressed he looked, to Keith's eye, even more like an ailing camel than usual.

They intercepted Deborah, on her way home from playing with her friend at the market garden but indignant that her *better* friend, Jean McLelland, had not joined them. She climbed cheerfully into the car, always ready for an outing. Munro stopped at Briesland House while Keith spoke to Molly. Keith joined Deborah on the back seat and they set off again.

'You remember coming out with me yesterday?' Keith asked.

'When we drove fast and had the accident?'

'You could put it like that.'

'I remember,' Deborah said.

'You probably know that something happened at the factory and people were hurt. We think that the bad men may have been watching to see where we went. If we all go back over the same roads, would you be very clever and remember who we saw and what cars we passed?'

64

Deborah might be young but, like all of her sex, she knew when she held trumps. 'If I remember something important, can I have ballet lessons?'

Keith waited, but Munro did not seem to have heard. 'We'll see,' Keith said, and he knew that, in retrospect, those words would be construed as a binding commitment. 'Yesterday,' he said, 'the first time we came along this way, was anybody following us?'

Deborah shook her head. 'Mr Ledbetter's taxi passed us, going the other way,' she said, 'and I looked round to see who was in it.'

'Good girl,' Munro said over his shoulder.

'The lorry we'd passed was still behind us,' Deborah said. 'It had "Removals" painted on it.'

'She's a good reader,' Keith said proudly. 'You can scoot on through the town. If they weren't following me, they were watching from up on the main road.'

'They couldn't see you here,' Munro protested as the streets closed round them.

'True. But the west side's all houses and occupied shops. The kind of places I might have been going to are all up Canal Street or View Street, and they could have watched me all the way if I'd turned up in that direction.'

'They could have been waiting for you at the edge of the town.'

'Did anybody follow us through the town?' Keith asked Deborah.

'No.'

'That settles that,' Keith said. 'We'll head for the factories.'

'This is all very well,' Munro said. 'But you're assuming that the criminals had access to a great deal of local knowledge.'

65

'It sticks out a mile that that's exactly what they had.'

Munro thought it over so intensely that he nearly went through a pedestrian crossing on a red light. He braked just in time. 'Doig will be pulling in the local crooks for questioning, but there are none in this league.'

'I don't see them opening their mouths to Doig,' Keith said. 'You can move on now. I'd guess that they bribed some local small fry. I'll try to find out through somebody who owes me a favour.'

'Small crooks shouldn't owe gunsmiths favours,' Munro said indignantly.

'Dougie Scott does, remember? My evidence got him off a poaching charge. I know he's usually guilty as hell, but this time he wasn't.'

They were nearing the industrial estate. Munro slowed right down. 'I don't want to be seen around here,' he said, 'and in your company.'

'Stop at the road mouth if you can,' Keith said. 'If not, drive on and find somewhere less conspicuous to park.'

There was no police activity at the entry although the bright colours of police cars could be seen deep in the industrial estate. Munro parked, but he kept his engine running and his foot on the clutch.

'Relax,' Keith said. 'There's no law says you can't chauffeur me around while my car's in dock, even if you have slipped a disc. What are friends for? Listen, Deb. We turned in here, remember? I spoke to the policemen and we came out again. Was anybody hanging around?'

'Nobody.'

'Anybody with the cars?'

'There was a van outside that place.' Deborah pointed to the loading bay of a packaging factory. 'Just as we were leaving, a man came out and started putting boxes into it.'

66

'Sure that's all?'

'Quite sure.'

'Right. So we came back here and stopped, ready to turn the way we're facing now. Who did we see?'

Deborah's small face screwed up in effort. 'Sir Peter's big, old car went by. I looked after it, and Mrs Bruing was getting into her Mini outside the Spar shop. A few ladies were pushing prams or walking with dogs. But I didn't notice who they were,' Deborah added anxiously.

'Doesn't matter. Drive on, McDuff, but slowly. Deborah, we're just coming to the really important bit. We came out this way. What did we see?'

'There was a little white sports car. A Spridget.'

'So there was!' Keith said. 'About here. A girl was driving. A farmer's daughter from somewhere south of the town.'

'You couldn't get by at first,' Deborah said. 'Mr McLelland was coming the other way with his tractor and trailer, fetching straw bales. Then you went whizzing along. Whizzing along,' she repeated.

Superintendent Munro did not take the hint but maintained his usual sober pace. 'What next?' he asked.

Deborah sighed. The trip was turning out to be much less exciting than she had hoped. 'I don't remember anything else until three cars came round the bend from the main road. First there was another Mini. I think it was the one which parks in the square, but it wasn't the usual man driving, it was a woman.'

'It is a *big* car we're wanting to know about,' Munro said.

'Let her tell it in her own way. But, Deb, you mustn't say "woman". Say "lady".'

'Then there was a Beetle,' Deborah said, 'and there was an old man driving it. He was going slow. Behind that there was a big car which seemed to want to get past the Beetle but it had to wait until we'd gone by. It had a whole lot of people in it.'

'Men?'

'I think so, all except the driver. A lady was driving.'

'Could there have been as many as six people in the big car?' Keith asked.

Deborah looked down at her fingers and then nodded uncertainly. 'I think so,' she said.

Munro stopped the car and reversed into a field-gate rather than arrive again within sight of the road-block. 'That was all?' he asked.

Keith reworded the question. 'There was nobody else as far as the main road?'

'No, Dad.'

'And in the main road we only saw two big lorries?'

'And we nearly hit one of them,' Deborah said with enthusiasm.

'But not quite,' Keith said. He had been trying to forget the incident. He met Munro's eye in the mirror.

'Your guess sounds good,' Munro said. 'At least there was a big car in a hurry, full of men. It is the woman driving I don't like.'

'How did you know that it was a woman?' Keith asked Deborah.

'She was like Mrs Beattie. That's what made me look at her.'

'Mrs Beattie, your teacher? Square face. Straight, dark hair. About as tall as your mum, but stout. Like that?'

'Yes.'

'She couldn't have been a man with long hair?'

Deborah shook her head. 'She had a lot of bosom, just like Mrs Beattie. And I saw her again later and she was wearing a skirt.'

'When?' both men said together.

'Aunt Janet took me up to the flat while she made their tea. I was looking out of the kitchen window. She walked along the back lane, from Birch Street towards The Avenue.'

'From your right to your left?' Keith caught Munro's eye in the mirror again. 'She was walking south, towards here. That could make sense.'

'It would, if she had just dumped a stolen car and was heading towards a rendezvous.' Munro agreed. 'Could the lassie describe the car?'

'Can you, Toots?'

'It was big,' Deborah said. 'Sort of brown. About the colour of Mr Smiley's new Range Rover.'

'Bronze,' Keith said. 'An excited man could mistake it for red.'

'What about the make?' Munro asked.

'She'd be guessing. Let's head back into the town and see whether she recognises any shapes.'

They visited two small carparks but saw nothing, according to Deborah, resembling the large, bronze car. The parking spaces in the square were almost full. Munro tucked himself and his car into a quiet corner and waited. Keith took his daughter's hand and walked her round while she studied the larger cars from the front and side. Suddenly, she stopped. 'Like that blue one, but boxier at the back.'

They returned to Munro's car. 'Granada Estate,' Keith said, 'or something very like it.'

'If only the rest of the public were as observant,' Munro said. 'We shall have to breed from the wee one.'

'No doubt we will, but let's get her safely married first. Do you have enough to get you out of the muck?'

'It just might do the trick,' Munro said.

69

Superintendent Munro escorted Deborah up to the flat over the shop where, with the help of Janet James, he made sure that he was in possession of every detail that she could be induced to remember. Then, limping theatrically and leaning on a stick borrowed from Wallace, he went to visit his former friend, Chief Superintendent Doig.

Keith, meanwhile, had borrowed the superintendent's car. Dougie Scott did not rank among Keith's friends and only marginally among his acquaintances, but Keith had heard the old rogue's address read out in court and the name New Row had stayed in his memory. A few enquiries in that short and unattractive cul-de-sac brought him to the door of a scruffy cottage where a stout and cheerful woman with purple hair told him that Dougie was 'up Deer Hill'.

That was all that Keith needed to know. He drove a couple of miles into the hills east of the town, left the car among a screen of trees and took to his feet. He knew the ground well and knew enough of Dougie Scott to make an accurate guess as to where he would find him. His way climbed through stubble and uncultivated grazing land onto heather, and he came gently over the crest. Sure enough, a squat figure showed up. Dougie was crouched comfortably, his back against a boulder, where the whole southern slope of the hill and the country beyond was laid out before him. In his right hand he held the old, brass binoculars through which he was studying the scene, while with the other hand he was fondling the head of a grizzled lurcher.

Keith walked very softly. What breeze there was was in his face and neither man nor dog sensed his presence until he spoke.

'Hullo, Dougie.'

70

The dog would have gone for him, but the man stopped it with a sharp word. If Dougie Scott was surprised he was too well-schooled a villain to show it. He was a coarse man, pot-bellied but fit-looking, dressed in a filthy old macintosh and a tweed fishing hat.

'Well, Mr Calder,' he said calmly. He puffed a large and battered pipe and waited.

Keith seated himself on an outcrop of rock. 'What in God's name are you smoking?' he asked.

Dougie smiled faintly. 'My own mixture.'

'I bet. It smells as if it'd do you more good spread under your rhubarb. But each to his taste. Dougie, I want your help.'

'Ah!' Dougie nodded slowly. 'I told you I was obliged to you, and I am.'

'I only told the truth,' Keith said. 'I saw the dog that killed the deer and it wasn't yours.'

Dougie dropped a hand to the dog's neck. 'I don't use old Speedy to run down deer. But there's many wouldn't have bothered to speak up for him. They'd've let an old dog be put down before his time.'

'Were you up here yesterday?'

'No harm in that, is there?'

'Some,' Keith said. 'But I'm not greatly concerned if you were spying out the movements of the deer, in preparation for a foray at dawn or dusk. That may be my brother-in-law's business, but it's not mine and I won't tell him if you don't. He likely knows, anyway.'

'It's no crime to watch the deer,' Dougie said. 'He'd need to catch me with a poached beast. And he'll never do that. Old Speedy's past it now, poor old lad. We're both ageing, only fit to sit in the sun and watch the deer go by.'

Keith suppressed a grin. The pathos had been

71

consummately artistic. 'And no way would you get a firearms certificate, with all those convictions behind you. Right?'

'That's right.'

'You old sinner,' Keith said. 'I ken damn fine you've got an old army rifle hidden away somewhere, quite illegal and off-certificate. Did you think I couldn't guess why your pal McFlodden bought three-o-three ammunition on his own certificate after he'd bulged the barrel of his own three-o-three and put it away?'

Dougie played a little tune on his pipe. 'You going to make trouble for me, Mr Calder?'

'Not if you help me out,' Keith said. 'There was a lorryload of guns stolen yesterday. You heard about it?'

'Everybody's heard that, Mr Calder. A bad business. Two men died, so I've heard. I knew one of them.'

'A blue articulated,' Keith said, 'although it's possible that the trailer already had camouflage paint on it. You'd have been watching the deer tracks, but you couldn't have missed a thing like that on the Oldbury Farm road or the forestry tracks.'

Dougie thought it over while he puffed furiously on his pipe. Keith began to wonder whether he was sending smoke-signals, and leaned aside to evade the worst of the pollution.

'Nothing like that,' Dougie said at last.

'I didn't expect it,' Keith said. 'If they came this far it would likely have been after dark. You've seen nothing suspicious yesterday or today?'

'I've not seen a soul but foresters. And a wagon-load of sheep.'

'The hijack was carefully planned,' Keith said. 'They seem to have had a lot of local knowledge. During the past month or so, has any stranger been spying out the

72

land or asking questions?'

'Not that I've seen or heard.'

'Then somebody local has been acting as their consultant.'

'Not me, Mr Calder.'

'Of course not you,' Keith said impatiently. 'You're too small a fish to swim with the sharks. But you're on nodding terms with everybody on the shitty side of the law around these parts, and I've seen you coming out of High Tavern, which is where every disreputable character goes to do his boozing. So go and chat with your crookeder friends. Listen. Ask questions but be careful. See if you can't find out who's been helping an outside gang with local information. Do that for me and I'll see if I can get you into some legitimate deer control. But, if you cross me, there may come another time when you'll look round suddenly and find me there, and you won't care for it at all.'

Dougie smiled, showing gaps in his yellow teeth, and knocked his pipe out on his heel. 'Another time,' he said, 'you'd not have the smell of my tobacco to guide you. Well, I'll see what I can find out. I'm not doing it for threats or bribes, mind, but because one of those lads, Willy Fife, is my cousin's son. Instead of deer control, though, could you get me taken on as an assistant keeper for three months?'

'Maybe I could,' Keith said. He knew that there is no keeper to match a reformed poacher, but he would have to do some fast talking to persuade any estate or shooting tenant to let Dougie Scott within a mile of their pheasants.

'Just three months, mind,' Dougie said. 'To renew my Benefit.'

73

SEVEN

Molly was unable to express by more than a lifted eyebrow her irritation at the sudden task of providing dinner for nine. Keith was sometimes given to impulsive hospitality, but when Molly had once protested she had found herself disarmed by the presentation of a microwave oven and a well-stocked deep-freeze.

When the Calders saw from the dining room window that Ronnie had brought Butch as an extra and uninvited guest, Molly felt free to utter a wordless exclamation of disgust.

'I'm not too pleased either,' Keith said. 'I'd been hoping to keep out of Butch's way until the shit stopped flying.'

'Well, you'll have to make do with a shaving off everybody else's steak, or go vegetarian. The freezerman's due next week.'

'Maybe she won't stay to eat.'

'I should be so lucky!' Molly said. 'She's dressed for dining out.'

'Take my steak and fry me some sausages,' Keith suggested.

'What sausages?'

Ronnie ushered his lady in. He was looking subdued

and with good reason. Butch was, as Molly later put it, 'Up to high do'. Superintendent Munro arrived only seconds behind them, so Keith left the two ill-assorted men to entertain each other and herded the fulminating Butch into his study. He pulled out two chairs, and when she remained obstinately standing he sat down, not behind his desk where he might seem to be taking shelter but out in the open.

'You lose my damn guns,' was her opening shot.

'I didn't lose them,' Keith said reasonably. 'I never received them. The whole damn lorry was stolen.'

'No matter. They were in your charge.' In her agitation, she set off around the room in a clockwise direction. 'You make a ball-up. I sue. I sue the hell out of you.'

Keith ducked as she passed behind him, but for the moment her attack was only verbal. 'I didn't guarantee safe delivery,' he said. 'I told you – in writing – that your boxes could have space on the lorry if you wanted it, but that it was up to you to take out insurance. So you wouldn't get anywhere in court. *Did* you insure?'

She had paused to listen to him, but now she set off again, anticlockwise this time, her athletic, dancer's stride carrying her over the carpet so fleetly that the wind of her passing ruffled his hair. 'What that does with it?' she demanded. 'I not want insurance, want my bleedering guns. That . . . that wagon was to be protected.'

'It was.'

'Some protecting!'

'Four policemen were guarding it,' Keith said. 'One was killed.'

She stopped in her tracks and blinked at him. 'I hear this,' she said. 'Is bad. Is bloody awful, but does not make losing my guns less worse. Guns were not mine

75

only. Belong to a . . . a group.'

'A consortium?'

'I suppose. But I . . . I have responsibletitty. If my arse is on block, why should you be off bloody hook? If court of law not clobber you, I . . . I clour living fuck out of you,' she finished with gusto.

'Sit down,' Keith said, 'and let's discuss this reasonably.'

The use of that part of Ronnie's disreputable vocabulary which he had so far conveyed to her seemed to have relieved her feelings, but instead of sitting down she went to look out of the window. The low sun struck through her dress as if it had been muslin, revealing every detail of her figure. Keith, usually, would have looked his fill with a comfortable feeling that he was stealing an advantage. But Butch knew exactly what she was doing and he had a feeling that if any advantage was to be stolen she was the girl to do it. He fixed his eyes firmly on a corner of the ceiling.

'What to discuss?' she asked abruptly. 'You lose my guns, I kick up shit.'

'That's agreed,' Keith said. 'Now let's go and have a drink.'

'What you *doing* about it?' she demanded. 'Ronnee tell me you are damn good at recovering lost guns, buy this house with rewards from insurance companies.'

'Ronnie talks too damn much,' Keith said. 'But yes, I'm doing all I can to find the damn things. It might help if you told me who, in this country, knew about them.'

'The crew of the *Mazorian*, and you and Ronnee, is all.' She spun round suddenly and caught him peeping. 'Any other body, they learn it from you.' She was looking smug.

'I fixed the transport through the man who owns the

76

rest of the load,' Keith said. 'And my partner knew, of course. That's all.'

'Is too many. And if you get guns back, how I know you don't keep them yourself?'

It was not like Keith to dislike conversing with a pretty girl who was showing off her figure to him, but this was one such occasion. 'Ronnie can keep you posted,' he said stiffly. To his great relief, he heard Molly calling them through for their meal. He got up.

'Is right,' she said slowly. 'Ronnee not let you swick me.'

She preceded him out of the room. Keith kept his eyes off her rump. He knew what it looked like anyway.

The rest of the working party were already assembled and discussing, in suitably shocked tones, what the papers were already calling the 'Gunjack Massacre'. Ronnie and the superintendent were neat in tweed suits; Wallace, Keith's partner, very much the businessman in sober pinstripe; Wallace's wife Janet, golden as always, in something pale; Mrs Enterkin, plump and charming in something dark; Sir Peter Hay, untidy in his best kilt; Molly, flushed from cooking, hastily changed into what Keith recognised as her best cocktail dress; Deborah, unusually clean and shiny; and another unexpected guest, Mr Enterkin, the solicitor, plump as his wife and looking embarrassed.

Ronnie had taken over Keith's duties as host and dispensed drinks with a generous paw. Keith provided Butch with a large gin, and himself with a much-diluted malt whisky. He would have preferred to get his fair share of his own drink, but a clear head would be needed that night.

Molly called them to table. Even with all the leaves in, it was a tight squeeze. While they were milling around,

Mr Enterkin took Keith aside. 'I came only as chauffeur,' he said. 'Your good lady insisted that I remain.'

'Quite right,' Keith said. 'We may need a good lawyer before this is over.' He could guess who was next in line for short rations. Molly, however, had made up the portions with kidneys and bacon. Keith, who had eaten nothing since his late breakfast, felt ready to dribble down his chin.

Deborah monopolised the conversation at first; not at the wish of her parents, who did not believe in such indulgence, but because she was unstoppable. She recounted at length her own major contribution. Chief Superintendent Doig had collected her personally from the shop, and it seemed that she had declaimed at length before an admiring throng of senior officers. Ballet was forgotten. What she now wanted was her own Identikit set.

Butch had not got the whole of her grievance off her chest and by the time the sweet was on the table she had managed to take over the conversation with a recital of her troubles.

Mr Enterkin, who enjoyed the sound of his own voice, was not a man to accept a silent role. When Butch paused for breath and to take food, he took over. 'Miss Baczwynska's loss raises an interesting point,' he said. 'Was the robbery committed for the antique guns or for the modern, for the arms as arms or for the cash value of both? Keith, which consignment would have been the more valuable?'

Keith shrugged. Any figure which he mentioned now would be pounced on and become a firm valuation, later appearing in the press; this he knew from bitter experience. 'The value of anything is only what the next fool to come along can be induced to pay for it,' he said.

'You mentioned figures this morning,' Munro said.

'Those were off the top of the head,' Keith said. 'I wouldn't want to be quoted on them.'

Mrs Enterkin leaned forward to speak down the table to him. 'But you value guns every day,' she said in her soft, West Country voice. 'You must be able to put a figure on them.'

'I haven't seen any of them yet,' Keith said.

'Mine are very good,' Butch said. 'What you call mink.'

'Mint,' Keith said. 'I could make a guess on that basis, and if they really are mint and if we don't hurry the selling I wouldn't expect to be very far out. But if there isn't a collector or a museum waiting for a particular gun with the money in his fist, we either drop the price or we have to wait. On the black market, without provenance, I doubt if thieves would get a tenth as much.'

'What about the modern guns?' Molly put in.

'Depends who you are,' Keith said. 'Look at it this way. The biggest arms warehouse in Britain is in Manchester. If you have four hundred thousand to spend you can walk in and buy a Centurian tank, fully armed and in good working order. They might even give you a trade-in on your old one. But if you're a government suffering an arms embargo, say South Africa, you're in a different game. By the time it's been bought through the Middle East and trans-shipped at Marseilles, and everybody along the line has had a cut, it might cost you a million.

'On a smaller scale, it's even more complicated. Each of those Brownings, new or in perfect order, has a legitimate price of about a hundred quid. The Sterlings, slightly more. If you wanted to buy a pistol to knock off – ' Keith paused. He had been about to say *your brother-in-*

law, which would have been a Freudian slip and the end of an imperfect friendship ' – your worst enemy,' he resumed, 'you'd pay several times that value. After you'd done the deed, if you were fool enough to want to sell it instead of dropping it into the nearest loch, you'd be lucky to get a fiver for it.'

'But,' he went on, 'knowing Eddie, I doubt whether his guns were much better than junk. As new, that load would be worth about the half-million which I mentioned to Mr Munro today. If Eddie undercut the bigger dealers, I'd guess that he quoted about four hundred thousand. The guns probably cost him about a third of that. He'd be expecting to spend about another third on transport and on our costs for overhauling them, the remaining third covering his profit and the overheads of his business. That's one way of looking at the figures. On the other hand, sold to a revolutionary army or into organised crime, they could realise a whole lot more. And that's not counting the value of the ammunition which was on the lorry, because I don't know how much there was.'

'You seem,' said Mr Enterkin, 'to be evading the question put by my fiscally-minded wife.'

'I'll say this much and then we'll drop the subject,' Keith said. 'On the legitimate market, the antiques might have approached the modern guns in value. Once stolen, the value of the modern guns would go up, the antiques down.'

Superintendent Munro had been eating in silence, but now he looked up. 'From the time when it could have been known that the antiques were on that vehicle,' he said, 'until the time of the attack, there would not have been enough time to do the necessary planning and to put together a team with such professional ruthlessness.'

'Unless the team were already assembled for some other purpose,' Mr Enterkin suggested.

'I prefer,' said the superintendent, 'to believe that the modern guns were the target all along. And I do not seem to be alone in my belief. I hear that Special Branch are on the scene already and actively observing a number of persons who appeared within hours after the robbery and murders.'

'That was going to be my news,' Mrs Enterkin said, 'and now you've stolen my thunder. Two different groups are staying at the hotel. They keep themselves very much to themselves. Their names and passports are British, their accents would get by, but sometimes they give themselves away over little things like the value of the new coins or how to use the telephones. It's the same in the other hotels, I hear.'

'That makes sense,' Keith said. 'The hijack was public knowledge more than twenty-four hours ago. It wouldn't take the embassies long to get their men here.'

'I don't understand,' Molly said plaintively. 'What embassies? Who are these people? Why does it make sense?'

'Look at it like this, Mrs Calder,' said the superintendent. 'There is only one good market for the stolen guns, and that is a group of – well, call them terrorists or freedom fighters, it depends on your point of view. So there are two possible motives. Such a group siezed them for their own use, or some criminals wanted the guns to sell to that group. Consider, for example, the P.L.O. They have been disarmed and scattered, but their leaders have ready access to finance. To rearm and regroup, they need a large source of purchased or stolen guns. When the news broke that a large consignment of guns had been stolen, Mossad would have men here

81

immediately, to watch and wait and if necessary to take action, to ensure that those guns did not end up in the hands of the P.L.O. Conversely, unless the guns were stolen by or for the P.L.O., they would send their men in the hope of making contact with the thieves and buying them.'

'Substitute any other subversive group and its opponents,' Wallace said, 'and you have the same story.'

'I was in the George at lunchtime,' Ronnie said. 'There's two strangers putting up there, I was told, and a mannie was saying he'd heard them talking Russian to each other.'

'And how would he be telling Russian from Polish, say, or Turkish or Czech?' Munro asked.

'If they was Russians,' Butch said darkly, 'likely they here to be sure guns do not go to Afghans.'

Molly paused in the act of pouring coffee. 'Has it reached the stage where we're really, seriously, talking about Russian spies?' she asked. 'For Heaven's sake, Keith, how is it all going to end?'

'Probably with a bloody great bang,' Keith said. 'Unless the police get there first, I can see the first on the scene destroying the lot just to prevent it falling into the hands of whoever they see as their opposition. Don't get all het up,' he added quickly as Molly turned pale. 'I was mostly joking and, anyway, we're not going to be that close. All we're trying to do is to help Mr Munro to look better, and help the police to find Butch's guns. We won't stand too near.'

'I've heard that before,' Molly said.

Butch found her voice again. 'But if somebody blow up guns, they not look to see which are antics. They blow up whole lot. What we do? We offer reward?'

'That could help,' Keith said. 'Could you afford to

offer a reward?'

'*You* offer reward! We refund when guns sold.'

Keith glanced at Wallace, the money man. Wallace shook his head firmly. 'You could raise money on the prospect of selling the guns,' Keith told Butch. 'I could give you a provisional valuation to support the loan. After all, if you don't get them back you don't pay out the reward.'

Before Butch could launch herself into another tirade of grumbles, Molly cut in. 'Time for your bath,' she told Deborah.

'Can I have a story?'

'You've heard enough stories today.'

'But, Mum . . . .'

'No nonsense,' Keith said sternly. 'Off you go. And, remember, not a word to anybody about anything you've heard in this room today.'

'Not ever?'

'Not until I tell you.'

Deborah thought it over and then nodded. 'All right,' she said. 'Will Butch come up and see me dance?'

'Not this time, my darling,' Butch said. 'I need myself here.'

'Come down and say goodnight when you're ready,' Molly said, taking her daughter to the door. Keith's heart turned over, as it so often did when he saw the two of them as a unit of mother-and-child, symbolising all that had ever been comforting in his own life. Molly, mother of a piece of himself, returned and sat down. Keith could feel a new mood descend. This group, or others very like it, had tackled and solved many problems in the past despite, or perhaps because of, their diversity of knowledge and background. Whatever the question, somebody would know the answer or where to go for it.

'Now,' Keith said. 'Paul York will be here soon, so let's see if we've covered the ground.'

'I mustn't meet York,' Munro said. 'What do we do while he's here?'

'I'll see him alone in the study,' Keith said. 'It was once a dining room before we changed the house around, and there's a hoist down to the utility room which used to be the kitchen. The hoist's a cupboard now, but if I leave its door ajar anyone who wants to can hear every word.'

Munro nodded satisfaction. 'Now I'll bring you up to date,' he said. 'In following up the information supplied by your wean, a bronze Granada Estate was discovered, parked behind the Town Hall.'

Sir Peter Hay had spent the meal listening with the rapt air of a theatre-goer, but now he broke his silence. 'Does this not let you off the hook, Superintendent?' he asked.

'I realise that I am being a trouble and an expense to you all,' Munro said. 'And I appreciate –'

'My dear chap,' Sir Peter said quickly, 'I didn't for a moment mean to imply that you weren't welcome to any help it was in my power to provide. It just seemed to me that you've done what you set out to do. You've found a witness who has contributed to the investigation. Surely that gives Chief Superintendent Doig a good reason to make a favourable mention of your zeal and intelligence in his report?'

'That would depend,' Munro said. 'The car was stolen, as it turns out; but because the owner is abroad, it would not have been reported stolen until he looked for it on his return. So the car was not on the stolen list. It can't be denied that, with some help, I've produced the car before it would otherwise have been found, and if it provides useful information then I think that the blot on my record will be cancelled. The lads from Forensic will be making all the usual tests, and I have passed on the suggestion that paint might have been carried. But if nothing comes of their work, then I'm still under a cloud. I'd be grateful . . .'

'We won't stop until we're sure,' Keith said. 'One way or the other,' he added. It never did to let Munro get over-confident. 'Any other news?'

Munro shook his head.

'Then we'll go round the table, although it's too early to expect much.' Briefly, he told them of his talk with Dougie Scott on Deer Hill. Then he turned to Janet on his left.

'No word yet of a stranger asking questions,' she said, 'but we've put the word around and something may come back. We've found an angler who was after trout in Skelly Burn. He didn't see anything.'

'He wouldn't,' said Ronnie, who was on Janet's left. 'That burn's in a deep gulley all the way. Me, I'm doing what you said. I've covered about half the ground, looking for traces, but I'm wasting Sir Peter's time.' He glanced at his employer.

'Never mind that,' Sir Peter said. 'Just finish the task.'

'If you say so. I've marked up your map, Keith, lad. So far, there's one place I've found which I can swear no heavy vehicle's crossed. Otherwise, I can't tell either way, let alone tell if one particular vehicle out of dozens has gone by. The ground's that baked.'

Keith's eye passed over Deborah's empty chair to Wallace. 'Janet's told it all,' Wal said.

'I'm only an interested observer,' said Mr Enterkin.

'So'm I,' said Molly.

85

Keith began to come down the other side of the table. He skipped over Munro, who had already made his report, and looked at Butch.

'I know nothing,' Butch said.

'Peter?'

'Nothing helpful, I'm afraid,' said Sir Peter. 'My two gangs of foresters were at work and a contractor had men doing a drainage job for me. They've all been contacted. The short answer is that nobody saw any vehicles that weren't fully identified. They've all been told to mark their locations on a map in the estate office, and from the marks so far made it doesn't look as if anything could have been east of the town and gone unseen.'

Keith hesitated and then moved on to Mrs Enterkin, who was sitting on his right. 'I've no more news,' she said.

'No rumours, even?' Keith asked.

'There's always rumours, but nothing to help. The one, steady rumour at the moment is that there was a conjuring trick, and the guns are already out of the district.'

'Surely,' Wallace said, 'there never was any doubt that the whole thing involves a trick of misdirection. I think it might help if Sir Peter got more details from his men. Firstly, details of the vehicles they saw, in case the lorry with the guns was seen, but had been disguised and wasn't recognised. And, secondly, where was each man *at what time?* Because there may still have been gaps.'

'Good points,' Sir Peter said. 'I'll put those two enquiries in hand.'

Discussion petered out and the others looked at Keith, who was staring vacantly at a point on the far wall. He came back to earth with a start. 'Misdirection,' he said. 'You've just made me realise that our chances are better

86

than we thought.'

'You mean worse, surely,' Sir Peter said.

'No, I mean better. Superintendent, I suggest you get your colleagues to contact the firm on Clydeside which hired Eddie Adoni the original vehicle. See whether they can account for all their artics.'

'I can do that,' Munro said. 'But why?'

'Because the vehicle which nearly shunted me off the road was very, very like the one the guns were in. I think it was a decoy. You were meant to go haring off after it. Probably it did a similar disappearing act, somewhere miles away. You'd have been left hunting for it among the Cheviots or some place, but for the chance that I was suspicious and warned you to guard the junctions.'

'That sounds likely enough,' Ronnie said. 'But can you – or any other body – tell me why it improves our chances?'

Mr Enterkin chuckled suddenly. 'I think I can,' he said. 'One thing has been sticking in my craw – and in that of the general public, to judge by the rumour quoted by my good lady – and that is the fact that, despite all you say, Keith, about camouflage and emptiness, the gang would surely be mad to keep a whole trailer and trailer-load of stolen guns here for any length of time. However good the hiding place and the misdirection, a protracted search by the police and associated helpers must surely discover it in the long run. But the point which Keith is making, if I understand him aright, is that it was never intended to be hidden around here for long. The hiding-place need only be good enough to withstand the first, cursory search. Then, when the police responded to reports of the vehicle being seen elsewhere, the real quarry could emerge from hiding in a fresh coat of paint, or with a new tarpaulin over the top, and head off in a different direction. As it turns out, however, the raiders find themselves caught in their temporary hiding-place for a much longer period than was ever intended. Am I right, Keith?'

'You are,' Keith said. 'Long-winded, but right.'

'If the reasoning is sound,' Munro said, 'and it certainly seems so, then a member of the public could happen on the vehicle at any time and find himself confronting a gang which already killed two men. I had better pass the word to Chief Superintendent Doig straight away.'

'You can phone from downstairs,' Keith said. He looked at his watch and then out of the window. 'Paul York is due, and car lights seem to be coming this way. Anybody who wants to stay and eavesdrop had better go downstairs quietly.'

EIGHT

Wallace and Mr Enterkin pronounced themselves ready to leave for home, but were overridden by their wives. The whole party vanished down into the basement, except Keith, who was left to admit the newcomer. He opened the front door as Paul York got out of Eddie Adoni's Volvo.

The two men greeted each other with no more than a nod. Keith led the way into the study and indicated a chair. The door of the cupboard, where the hoist had once been, was open, revealing bottles and glasses. York refused a drink. Keith made himself another dilute whisky and settled himself behind the desk. 'So what can I do for you?' he asked.

'You can tell me what you know so far.'

'You go first.'

Paul York looked blandly amused. 'You don't trust me, do you?' he said. 'I suppose that long streak of Highland misery you keep for a police superintendent around here has been damning me. All right, so I didn't cut it with the police. I was a good policeman and an honest one, whatever anyone may tell you, doing the job the way I saw it. The trouble was that in these enlightened days of love-thy-neighbourhood-crook-like-thyself-or-slightly-better, others didn't see the job the same way. I was out of step. Hints were dropped that I should quit the force, which I did. Since then, there have been rumours connecting me with other and worse things, but they're unfounded. You know how rumours can grow out of nothing.'

Keith knew how rumours could grow. He found himself almost ready to trust the big man. He respected his air of perfect fitness, and found something in his expression which he could not have defined but which told him that York and he could get along together. But, quite apart from Superintendent Munro's views, it was second nature to Keith to get as much as he could in exchange for as little as he need give. 'You may be a reincarnation of the original honest Injun,' he said. 'You still go first.'

York relaxed, just a little, although the largest chair in the room was still too small for his comfort. 'All right,' he said. 'Just to show good faith. Eddie's keeping a low profile, as they say, but this robbery has caught him on the raw. It's an enormous loss for him to take.'

'He was insured, wasn't he?'

'Not to anything like full value. His is a risky business and he's had losses in the past. The rate he was quoted was staggering, so he decided to carry most of the risk himself.'

'Has any reward been offered?'

'I thought we'd get around to that. Eddie's insurers have offered a reward for information leading to recovery, but only up to ten per cent of the insured amount. Eddie isn't joining in. He's pinning his faith on the police. But he wants blood, preferably yours or mine.'

'I don't see how he can rationally blame either of us,' Keith said mildly.

York gave a snort of mirthless laughter. 'If you think Eddie's always rational, you don't know him as well as I think you do. As far as he's concerned, I'm to blame for his incompetence. I shouldn't have let him keep me talking. I should have used the phone to delay the load. I should have caught up with it before it reached here.'

'And me?' Keith asked.

'Oh, if you weren't behind the whole thing you caused it by shooting your mouth off.'

This came as no great surprise to Keith. During his younger, wilder days it had been a local habit to credit him with more wild oats than he had ever sown, and that had proved to be one of the old habits that die hard. 'What do you think, yourself?' he asked York.

'Whether you talked or not doesn't matter; the shipment was known to far too many people anyway. I don't think you had any hand in the business; by reputation, you're tricky but not a crook.'

'Well, thank you very much,' Keith said.

'No sweat. What I'm saying is that we have a common interest in seeing the guns recovered. And each of us may have sources which Chief Superintendent Doig doesn't have and which we don't much fancy telling him about.'

'I see your lips moving,' Keith said, 'but I don't hear you saying anything. Why don't you pee or get off the pot?'

'God, I'd hate to play poker against you! All right,' York said without rancour, 'get ready. Here comes today's loss-leader. I have a useful source in the police. He gave me this. A witness has provided an Identikit picture, and the survivors have given estimates of the heights and weights of the men involved. Taking it all together, the police are ninety-nine per cent certain of the identities of the gang. Have you heard of Joyce's Boys?'

Keith sipped his drink while he thought back. 'There was something in the papers about a year ago,' he said. 'Some trial or other. The accused was said to be one of them. It was an English case and didn't get much coverage in Scotland. Am I right?'

'Quite right,' York said. 'He –'

The telephone bell cut off the sentence. Keith picked it up. Rapid pips denoted a call-box. He heard coins dropping.

'Mr Calder? This is Dougie Scott.'

'Hullo,' Keith said. 'How are you getting on?' He kept his eyes on Paul York, who was too obviously not listening. Keith pressed the receiver tight to his ear. York's expression changed minutely and Keith strained to interpret it.

'Mr Calder, I've been doing what you wanted and I think I've got something for you –'

It dawned on Keith that Paul York was looking satisfied when he should have shown frustration. 'Don't tell me on the phone,' he said. 'Call in and see me in the morning.' And he disconnected without giving Dougie a chance to protest.

The tiny shifts of expression were so small that Keith was depending on intuition as much as on his eyes, yet he thought that York's satisfaction had been replaced by annoyance. But York resumed as if the interruption had not occurred.

'He got off, in case that's of any interest. Do you remember Samuel Henshaw?'

This time, Keith was granted instant recall. The case had been an international *cause célèbre*. 'Professional assassin,' he said. 'London-born. He was killed in a gun-battle with the Marseilles police, some seven or eight years ago.'

92

'Joyce is his widow. Joyce's Boys is or are a singularly vicious gang, who seem at the moment to be missing from their usual London haunts. Joyce acts as their brains-cum-driver. They set up their own operations as a rule, but they're available at a price; and the whisper in London is that they went north to earn a fee.'

Keith gave a low whistle.

'That seems to be fair comment,' York said. 'Your turn next, but before you go ahead I'll tell you something else for nothing. If you ever bump into Joyce's Boys and you have to start shooting, shoot Joyce first. They're all dangerous, but she's the most dangerous of the lot.'

Keith felt that he was in a card-game. He had only a few low cards, while York held a fistful of trumps. But Keith wanted to see those trumps. 'This Joyce,' he said. 'Would she be of medium height with a square face, straight, dark hair, stout and with a big bust?'

York sat up straight. 'That's Joyce. Where've you seen her?'

'Somebody like that was driving a carful of men towards the factory just before the hijack. The car was probably a bronze Granada Estate. A stolen car of that type turned up in the town.'

'I knew about the car,' York said, 'but it's interesting to have Joyce confirmed. Not that there was much doubt. This has her trademark stamped all over it.'

'Tricky, is she?' Keith asked casually.

'Very. Simple things but effective. They cleaned out a jeweller's last month. The police received dozens of bogus calls to other shops, banks and post offices. By the time they'd worked out which call was genuine, the Boys were far away.'

This suggested another low card for Keith to play. He told York about the supposed decoy vehicle and the

93

chance which had negated its effectiveness. 'The superintendent is going to see if there isn't a clue in the hirings of the same firm,' he finished. And if York cared to assume that he was referring to the chief superintendent, then that would hardly be Keith's fault.

'You'll let me know if it leads anywhere?' York asked.

'Yes, of course. Now, tell me something.' Keith's voice held a gentle implication that he rather than York had been divulging all the hard news. 'I can guess who the original purchaser is or was. Is he still keen or has he gone cold on the deal? Could this whole operation have been his ploy to get them cheaper?'

'Joyce and her Boys don't come cheap,' York pointed out. 'And, yes, he's still keen. His agent was on the phone while I was in Eddie's office, and Eddie was turning somersaults to convince him that the deal was still on, even if Eddie had to make a new lot of guns himself in the back bedroom. I'm exaggerating, but that was the general effect. Over to you.'

Keith was running out of news with which to bargain. 'This was carefully set up,' he said, 'and timed to the minute. What rocked the boat for them was that the change of destination, which I'd given you several days earlier, didn't reach them and they only found out that there was a change at all when the load was on its way. Which lets you out, by the way. One line that I'm following up is where did their local information come from.'

'Have you considered the labourers you hired to unload?' York asked.

'I've thought about them very hard,' Keith said, 'because I only got hold of their foreman the day before, to tell him about the change, and he only told them to meet him in the square and that he'd lift them to the place in his van. I heard him.'

'Well, then –'

'But,' Keith said, 'they were all victims. Who on earth would let himself in for a fatal or near-fatal bash on the head?'

'That would be a reasonable question if we were dealing with people who were reasonable as we understand reason. But we're not. Joyce's logic is quite untainted by human weakness and her Boys follow her lead absolutely. Your man wouldn't know that he was for the chop. But he'd seen somebody's face and that was enough. Rather than leave an indication behind by killing just one, they killed them all, or tried to. The penalty, after all, would be no more severe. That kind of ruthlessness occurs sometimes, and it's at its worst when it spreads through a whole group. They infect and compete with each other until a sort of corporate paranoia takes over. It's more common among terrorists, where there's an emotional motive as well, but it happens among criminals too. So, if you're playing games among the big boys,' York wound up, 'my advice would be to give what you've got to me or to the police, or both, and then crawl into a hole and pull it in after you.'

'Believe me,' Keith said, 'I'm not going within a mile of them.'

'Very wise. Police opinion seems to be that they've made Britain too hot to hold them, and they're after some quick money to take abroad. Anybody who gets in their way now is liable to get his head in his hands. What else have you got?'

Keith decided that he had nothing left with which to bluff. 'Damn all,' he said. 'And you?'

York hesitated and then shook his head. 'That's it,

95

then,' he said. 'But I have a feeling that you know more than you've told.'

Keith had a feeling that they both knew more than they had told, with the difference that what he, Keith, knew, he had yet to put his finger on. Somebody had said something . . . . 'I've told you all I can,' he said.

As they shook hands, York said, 'Please, please disbelieve any rumours about me. Accept that I'm on the side of the angels. When I was on the force, your name used to come up when guns were mentioned. And somebody would always say that before you pulled your horns in and married you'd had a hundred mistresses. Exaggerated?'

'Ridiculous,' Keith said. He would have put the figure rather higher, himself.

'I didn't believe it,' York said. 'Do me the favour of not believing tales about me.'

Up the shaft of the hoist, Deborah's voice sounded with awful clarity. 'Mummy, what's mistresses?'

Munro, Ronnie and Sir Peter lingered for a further discussion, but Keith was unable to concentrate. Now that identities had been attached to the faceless villains, the existence of a dangerous quarry had become a reality. The realisation that they might exterminate anyone who became dangerous to them was acutely disturbing, and when at last he followed Molly to bed he uttered a wordless prayer that, in broadcasting his enquiries, he had not sent anyone into danger.

The thought kept him restless far into the night, and dawn was not far off when he fell at last into deep sleep. Molly, who had been aware of his restlessness, slipped out of bed without waking him as soon as she heard Deborah stirring. Superintendent Munro's troubles were insignificant when compared to her husband's need for sleep. She fed the child and despatched her to play with her friend at the nearby market-garden. She took in the mail, the milk and the day's papers (which always arrived by hand of the milkman, who rather fancied her). She had her own breakfast and set about the morning's chores.

Keith was woken an hour later by the ringing of the bedside extension. He ignored it until it stopped when Molly took the call downstairs. But a few seconds later she put her head round the door and saw that he was awake.

'For you,' she said.

He picked up the extension and took it under the duvet where the light was less troublesome. 'Calder,' he said.

'Ah, Mr Calder, good morning.' It was a smooth, deep voice with a polished accent. 'My name is Smithers and I represent the true owner of the guns which have so recently and tragically gone amiss. He still hopes to complete the deal.'

'I haven't got them,' Keith said cautiously.

'We are aware of that,' said the voice. 'Otherwise, you would hardly have circulated word around the town that you are anxious for word of them.'

'You've heard that, have you?' Keith said.

'I imagine that the whole town knows it. And you have a reputation for wiping the eye of the police. I believe that to be the expression.'

Keith remembered his talk with Paul York. 'Greatly exaggerated,' he said. 'When you say the true owner . . .'

'Mr Adoni had already been paid the bulk of the sum due. And I am to tell you that a reward will be paid for information leading to recovery by the police.' Keith thought that the voice placed emphasis on the last three words, which suggested that Mr Smithers might be who he claimed to be. 'I shall be staying at Millmont House until the load is either recovered or deemed lost for ever.'

'How much of a reward?' Keith asked.

'Ten per cent is, I believe, the usual figure. And there is one more thing. Among the Brownings there should be a special one in stainless steel.'

'Un-numbered?' Keith asked. Un-numbered hand-guns are a status symbol among V.I.P.s.

'Naturally. His Excellency would particularly want that one recovered,' Smithers said. 'He would like to arrange for some personalised engraving on it.'

'What would he like? Two missionaries boiling a cannibal?' Keith asked before he could stop himself.

'I will suggest it. Good morning.'

'Wait a minute,' Keith said. But Mr Smithers had rung off. 'I was only joking,' Keith told the bedside clock. God, was that the time?'

Keith was finishing a hasty breakfast when there was a ring at the door. 'It will be for you,' Molly said.

'Not necessarily,' Keith said, but he went to the door. There was a car in the drive and on the doorstep a tall man in a macintosh, hat in hand.

'Mr Calder?' he said. 'I'm from the *Glasgow Post*, covering the arms hijack and murders. My paper would pay handsomely for a tip-off on the whereabouts of the guns or the criminals.'

'If I knew anything like that, I'd tell the police,' Keith said. He had had some experience of reporters, and this man was too well-dressed and too urbane. 'How do I know you're a reporter?'

'If you're in any doubt, you could phone my editor. But whoever I am, I can still make it worth your while to give me your story. Do you have any idea as to where

they might be hiding? Or where they got their information?'

Keith decided that an evasive answer was called for.
'Fuck off,' he said, and slammed the door.

Ignoring repeated ringing of the doorbell, he picked
two envelopes off the mat and carried them back to the
kitchen. Each was addressed by hand and unstamped.

'Who was it?' Molly asked.

'One of the foreign spies, I think,' Keith said. 'Just
ignore him.'

One of the envelopes was addressed to 'Mr and Mrs
Calder', so he passed it to Molly as he sat down. Molly
often complained that she rarely received letters, forget-
ting that she never wrote any. The other envelope,
grubby and addressed to himself in a barely literate
hand, he slit open.

It was from Dougie Scott.

*I did what you said and asked round. The only chiel round here as
been seen meeting strangers a lot lately was Ian Skinner they call
him Pig you'll mind he did 3 out of 7 for G.B.H. in Glasgow. He
was seen sevral times meeting a man in the lay-by on the main
road, same man diffrent car each time, may have been more often
of course.*

*Other thing is he hasn't been seen round for a few days. I dont
like it Im getting out back when this is over. If Ive helped
rememember your promis.*

D.S.

Scott evidently believed that Ian Skinner had helped
Joyce's Boys and had been put down for his trouble. But
Keith knew Skinner by sight and by reputation. He had
seen the squat figure, with its ill-matched brown hair and

yellow beard, within the last day or two. Had Skinner not been in the square when Deborah was examining cars the day before?

Keith looked up, frowning, and opened his mouth to make some comment. The sight of Molly drove all other thoughts from his mind. She looked, suddenly, ten years older. She had turned the colour of dirty snow and was leaning against the table as if about to collapse. A moment later, indeed, she dropped into a chair and curled almost into a foetal position, her arms crossed over her breasts and her head on her knees.

His first thought was that she was having a heart attack. He jumped to his feet and put a hand on her shoulders in case she had fainted altogether. The note which she had been reading was lying on the table beside a scrap of ribbon. He snatched it up with his other hand. It was clumsily printed in block capitals with a left-hand slope.

IF YOU WANT TO SEE YOUR DAUGHTER AGAIN IN ONE PIECE INSTEAD OF A LOT OF LITTLE BITS, STOP NOSEY PARKERING. CALL OFF ALL YOUR SPIES AND SAY NOTHING TO THE POLICE. ANY MORE ENQUIRIES AND WE'LL POST HER BACK TO YOU ONE PIECE AT A TIME, NOSE FIRST.
IF YOU'RE GOOD, WE MAY ALLOW YOU TO BUY HER BACK UNHURT. HAVE £25,000 READY IN USED NOTES.

The message hit Keith with as much impact as it had Molly. He sank, rubber-kneed, into a chair beside her and put his arms round her, to draw comfort as well as to give it. He closed his eyes against the sight of the words. 'Oh my God!' he croaked.

After a few seconds he felt Molly stir. 'Keith, what are we going to do?'

NINE

'This is a judgment on me,' Keith said hoarsely. 'It's my fault for getting involved. You're always telling me not to, and now I've done it once too often and brought this on us.'

He felt Molly shaking him gently. 'I told you to get involved,' she said. 'If it's anybody's fault it's mine. So stop thinking about whose fault it is. We couldn't have stood by and done nothing when something so terrible had happened close to us. Are we going to call the police?'

'Have they really got her?'

'They sent the hair ribbon which she had on this morning.'

Keith opened his eyes. He had stopped shaking. He found himself looking into Molly's eyes, which were wet with tears. In them he saw his own reflection and more. He could see that although she was at the limit of her strength she would hold up until the crisis was past. Then, he thought, they could crack up together.

'No police,' he said. 'You saw what they wrote. We can't take any chances. We'll have to do what they say.'

She was still in the circle of his arms, but she held his lapels and shook him again. 'You're not thinking.'

102

'I know,' he said. 'My mind's gone numb.'

'You must think,' she said. 'If we ever needed your mind, it's now.' She broke out of his clasp and stood up. Standing behind him, she began to rub his neck muscles in just the way which she knew relaxed him. She was clumsy, and he could feel shudders coming though her fingers. 'I heard what that man York told you last night,' she said. 'These people have gone so far that now they'll kill at the least sign of danger. Do you think they'd really let us have Deborah alive once she's been in their hands, seen their faces and heard them talking?'

'If we paid the money . . . .'

'No,' Molly said firmly. 'They'd take the money if they thought they could get away with it, and they'd keep her alive until then. But once they had it they'd kill her and whoever brought the money as well. No, Keith, if we want to see her . . . alive . . . again, we've got to do something or let the police do it.'

'No police,' Keith said again. 'Just Munro.' And hearing his own voice uttering one firm decision, he knew that he had accepted the unacceptable as a fact and was ready to wrestle with it. As both Munro and York had reminded him, he had faced such challenges in the past and had triumphed without the help of the police or even despite their active opposition. But this time, it mattered. This time, it was essential that he prevailed. And his heart sank, because every gambler knows that when he must win, that is the time when he will lose.

Keith pushed the thought aside. Already his mind was racing.

'Could Paul York help?' Molly asked.

'Maybe, but not yet. I think he's Special Branch.'

'He's *what?*' Molly said.

'Special Branch. The penny only dropped when

103

Dougie Scott phoned me last night and wanted to tell what he's told me in his note – which isn't much, by the way, and none of it good. And York couldn't hide a little gleam in his eye, which made me think of wiretapping. And I realised that he'd told me things which Munro didn't know yet, like the identity of the gang, but he didn't yet know things which the regular fuzz knew, like the fact that Joyce had been seen. That made him police, but not a regular, and working under cover. That adds up to Special Branch. Left the Lothian and Borders Police under a carefully fabricated cloud so that he could do infiltration work. And we definitely do not want Special Branch muscling in just yet. I'm going to phone around until I get hold of Ronnie or Munro, and one of them can pick me up somewhere private. We need more to go on.'

'If you go searching around and asking questions, you may make . . . make it worse,' Molly said. 'Couldn't we agree to pay them the money and then turn up at the meet prepared to be as bad as they are, and quicker?'

Keith had already considered and discarded the idea. 'We'll keep that for a last resort,' he said. 'There's too much risk that somebody may spook them in the meantime, and they decide to cut their losses and run.'

Molly shivered. 'And you're sure you don't have enough to work on already?'

'Not by a mile,' Keith said.

'Something you haven't recognised yet? You're sure?' she persisted. 'Nothing that Mr Munro said . . . or Paul York . . . or Dougie Scott . . . or Deborah?'

'No,' Keith said. 'Absolutely, definitely not. Unless . . .' He fell silent. Molly rubbed on. Keith's neck muscles, which had felt like iron bars, were slowly relaxing.

104

'You just might be right,' Keith said suddenly, getting up. 'We'll get Janet to fetch you and to keep you with her in the flat. It might help if you tried to look like me when she picks you up, just in case somebody's watching. Wear one of my coats and a hat pulled down, and sit on a cushion. Take a gun out of stock if it would help you to feel more secure. I'll keep in touch.'

'All right,' Molly said. She put up a brave face. 'I know you'll do everything possible. Just be careful. And don't forget one thing. I may not be as good as you are at puzzling things out, and putting myself inside the other person's mind, but, if the worst comes to the worst, I can shoot.'

'So you can.' Gratefully, Keith kissed his wife.

He left the house by the basement door, which opened into a small courtyard overlooked only by an impenetrable shrubbery. Round the corner of the garage, formerly a stable, he slipped across the back drive and took to an almost forgotten path which squeezed along between the shrubbery and the high garden wall. A narrow gate let him out into the wood. He could have followed a ride, but preferred to take a more difficult route through the trees. Soon he was hot and the midges were maddening him, but at least he could be certain that he was unobserved. He was very conscious of the weight of the huge Le Mat revolver that he had taken from among the collectors' items in stock. Its weight of three pounds and more was against it, but he had ammunition available to fill its chambers with nine rounds of .44″ cartridges and the central barrel around which the cylinder rotated with its single .65″ cartridge of heavy shot. The only holster which would take it was old-fashioned and it would be slow to draw, but once he had it out he would have fire-power. The weight under his armpit was balanced by the binoculars bumping on his opposite hip.

Once in sight of the Newton Lauder road he waited, merged with the shadow of a small larch. Superintendent Munro's car arrived, slowed and stopped. Keith still waited until the only other car in sight vanished around the far bend, before darting across the open verge and dropping into Munro's passenger seat. He slid down until only the top of his head was visible.

'Back through Newton Lauder,' he said, 'and up the hill to the canal bridge.'

Munro turned the car in the track which led to Keith's back drive and set off back towards the town. 'What's adae?' he asked. 'You're acting gey canny, and your message sounded urgent.'

'It was urgent all right,' Keith said. 'But wait until Ronnie's with us. It's not a story I want to tell twice. Sound your horn outside his cottage and he'll follow us.'

'I'll do that,' Munro said. 'Am I allowed to know where we're going?'

'We're going to see what we can see. Deborah –' Keith's voice nearly broke on the name '– told us where to look.'

'I don't call it to mind.'

'I didn't either until just now, but the more I think about it the more I'm sure I'm right. Trust me a little longer.'

'Of course.' Munro slowed and turned left. Keith could see the tower of the police building. They climbed for perhaps a minute. Munro slowed again and sounded his horn. Keith sat up; the danger area was past. Ronnie's Land Rover had fallen in behind.

'I have disturbing news,' Munro said. 'These people –

106

Joyce's Boys – were already high on the wanted list. They carried out a bank-raid in Salford two weeks ago. The raid was unsuccessful, but a teller and two passers-by were killed and a gun bearing fingerprints was dropped.'

'So,' Keith said, 'the gang have to get abroad and they know it, and this caper is a last-ditch attempt to get some money together?'

'That is how I see it. And they will be all the more difficult to handle.'

'That's for sure.' But Keith could see one crumb of comfort in the news. If Joyce's Boys failed to get money for the guns, they might be desperate enough for cash to follow up the chance of a ransom for Deborah . . . .

'Chief Superintendent Doig,' Munro said, 'is becoming convinced that the guns have been smuggled away already, disguised as a milk tanker or some such dissimilar vehicle. His investigations are being handicapped by the diversion of manpower into maintaining the road-blocks. When the first search finishes, tonight or early tomorrow, he intends to dispense with road-blocks, or so I'm told.'

'That doesn't give us long,' Keith said. 'Go right here.'

'Not long at all.' Munro turned off as instructed and began to nurse his car carefully around the potholes in an unmade road. 'Your friend Miss Baczwynska has been telephoning Sandy Doig about once an hour.'

'Well, she would,' Keith said. 'Pull off on the left here.'

Munro pulled onto a triangle of firm grass where his car would be partly screened by a small stand of hawthorns and rowans. They transferred to Ronnie's Land Rover. Keith took the middle seat.

'Take us up to where we got the woodcock last October,' Keith said.

Ronnie glanced at him curiously. 'Your day for what-d'you-call-it messages, isn't it?' he said.

'Cryptic,' said Keith.

'Cryptic messages, that's right. "Get hold of our thin friend from Shabost and tell him to pick me up where Fat Simon ran over the fox." What sort of way's that to talk?' He turned up a track, climbing diagonally up the side of a hill which cut off their view of the town.

'I had to be guarded,' Keith said. 'I think my phone's tapped, and we've got trouble. Deborah's been kidnapped.'

The Land Rover wobbled and nearly left the track.

'That's bad,' Munro said. 'Och, that's just terrible!'

Ronnie grunted agreement. 'The poor wee bairn,' he added. 'You think she's up here?'

'No.'

'Do you think the guns are up here?' Munro asked.

'Could you see an artic getting up here? They'd have had to use mules,' Keith said. And, indeed, the Land Rover was scrambling up a narrow, rocky track with the hillside falling away under the nearside wheels.

'Then why are we coming up here?' Ronnie asked.

'To look where Deborah told us to look. At least, I think she did. If I'm wrong, we're in dire trouble.'

They lapsed into silence. Ronnie nursed the Land Rover upwards until they were on a level with the surrounding hilltops. They left the Land Rover in a field-gate and crossed the edge of a rough pasture to where a plantation hung askew over the crest of the hill like a towel thrown carelessly over a rail. They climbed a fence. The superintendent tore his trousers but the other two were more practised at passing barbed wire. Keith led them, pacing uncomfortably across the ridges and furrows while forcing through the prickling branches, to

108

the furthest corner where he squatted down, screened by a fringe of low gorse.

'Look but don't show yourselves,' Keith said. He passed Munro his binoculars. 'You brought it?' he asked Ronnie.

His brother-in-law squatted down beside him and produced the most powerful of his several stalking telescopes. 'Look where?' he asked.

Munro, stiffer in his limbs than the others, had seated himself. 'It's a good question,' he said. 'There is a devil of a lot to look at. It is time you told us where to look.' He waved a hand at the expanse of view, which ranged from the south junction below and in front of them, up the valley to their right, past Newton Lauder until the valley and the visibility both faded among the hills to the north.

'We're looking at the farmland this side of the town,' Keith said.

'We could have seen it better from where we were yesterday.'

'I think that's the first mistake we made, being seen up there,' Keith said. 'That, and spreading the word too widely that we wanted information. The result was this letter.'

He handed Munro the anonymous note. Munro read it, frowning, with Ronnie seething over his shoulder.

'You're sure that this is not a trick?' Munro asked. 'They do have her?'

'I phoned the market-garden. She never arrived.'

'Tae hell!' Ronnie's speech always got broader as he became angry. 'The puir wee bairn! If ye ken whaur she is, tell's. Nae bugger'll keep me frae fetchin' her oot.'

'And both of you dead, likely,' Keith said. 'Super-intendent, let's just suppose that I know where she is. What would you advise me to do? Do I ignore the warning and go running to Chief Superintendent Doig?'

Munro looked for inspiration in the sky, high above the sunlit farmland. 'I don't know,' he said at last. 'It is a terrible decision to be making. My training insists that I advise you to come straight to the police. But it would depend on circumstances.'

'I'll put it another way,' Keith said. 'If I go to Doig and tell him where she is, and that hostages are being held in some particular place, what will he do?'

'He is not a fool,' Munro said, 'one who would rush straight there and knock on the door.'

'But would he surround the place and call on them to come out with their hands up?'

'Knowing, as he does, the identities of these people, he would be more likely to ask for help from some such body as the S.A.S.'

'I don't fancy that a lot either,' Keith said.

'They are very highly trained,' Munro said. He did not meet Keith's eye.

'But to do what?' Keith asked. 'Could we be sure that they would approach with stealth, with the safety of the hostages as the prime objective?'

Munro was looking very unhappy. 'The safety of hostages would be a high priority,' he said.

'But not the first?'

'It would have to take its place with the safety of their own men and the success of the operation.' Munro tried to bite off the last word.

Keith pounced on the slip. 'So, as far as they are concerned, the operation would be the capture of the criminals. They might decide to go charging in with stun grenades, sweeping each room with gunfire at waist level, half a second after shouting at the hostages to lie down. Have you thought of that?'

'That is possible.'

'And anyone who was slow or deaf or dazed by the stun grenades or tied to a chair could get killed?'

'It has happened,' Munro said with a helpless gesture. 'You know that it has.'

'Well, maybe that's the best we'll be able to settle for, but I'm not convinced yet.'

Ronnie eased himself into a kneeling position. 'If you'll not tell us where she is,' he said, 'we can't even think about it.'

Keith nodded and returned to Munro. 'You're not here as a policeman,' he said, 'you're here as a friend. If I tell you where the guns are, which is presumably where the men and Deborah are also, will you promise me that you'll say nothing until I tell you to?'

Munro opened his mouth and closed it again. Finally, he forced himself to speak. 'You have my word,' he said.

'Thank you,' Keith said. 'Ronnie, see what you can see around the buildings at Lairy Farm. Mr Munro, take a look at the fields. You see the newly-cut stubble, two fields left of the farm buildings?'

'Yes.'

'In the next field beyond it there's a root crop, spuds I think. The darker green. You see that?'

'Yes.'

'Which of those fields would you say was the larger?'

Superintendent Munro was puzzled but persevering. 'I'd say that they were much of a muchness. But what can that have to do with it?'

'I'll tell you,' Keith said. 'Bear with me. Where the potatoes are, Neill McLelland had his barley last year; and he stacked his straw bales pretty much where he's got them again this year. I built my hide against them, when I was shooting pigeon over decoys on his oilseed rape, so I remember them well. Just the same sort of bales, each about five feet in diameter and four feet thick. He had a stack two bales deep, about sixteen bales long and four bales high, something like a hundred and twenty bales altogether. This year, off the same sized field, his stack is five bales thick and longer with it. And a tarpaulin over the top. It's a thrifty farmer who takes that much trouble over barley straw.'

'He could have grown a longer-stemmed barley,' Ronnie put in.

'You saw it when it was cut,' Keith said. 'It was just the same height.'

'Because there's so many bales,' Munro said carefully, 'you think the trailer's hidden inside them? But the lassie said . . .'

'Exactly! Neill was hauling more straw bales to his farm when Deborah and I passed him that morning.'

'Maybe he just wanted extra straw.'

'What for?' Keith asked. 'He's no extra beasts to bed with it during the winter, which is about all a farmer uses the straw for. But he'd need about another sixty, just to close in the ends. His neighbour this side just cleared and drained some boggy land. It goes to pasture next year, but just now he's got extra straw and no need for it. He'll have straw for the asking.'

Munro sat and scratched his head for a minute. He took a look through Keith's binoculars and lowered them again. 'But how would a city-bred gang know all that?' he asked plaintively. 'Would the farmer be in it with them? Mr McLelland seems an upright man.'

'I'm sure that he is,' Keith said. 'When we picked Deborah up yesterday, she was complaining that his daughter hadn't turned up to play. To me, that suggests that the family's being held and only allowed outside one at a time.

'On the other hand, I had a note from Dougie Scott this morning. He says that Ian Skinner, the one they call "Pig", has been meeting with strangers. When he's out of jail, he's always scrounging round the farms for odd jobs or unwanted junk while keeping his eyes open for anything he can come back and steal later. He'd be just the man to provide that sort of information. Dougie thought that Pig had already been put down, having outlived his usefulness; but I think he's been lying low. I'm sure he was in the square when we looked for cars yesterday.'

'You're both right,' Munro said. 'He was in the square yesterday. But this morning we found him on the road below here. A hit-and-run.'

They were silent for a few seconds, in memory of the late 'Pig' Skinner. The epitaph was left to Keith. 'We'll manage without him,' Keith said. 'But what a thing to do, just in case he talked later!'

Ronnie lowered the telescope. 'That'd not be the reason,' he said. 'Not if they were quitting the country anyway. More likely it'd be to save having to pay him.'

'That's worse,' Keith said. 'Do you see anything down there?'

'Not a thing moving. Give me a little longer.'

Keith's worries redoubled. Lack of movement might mean that the men had pulled out, leaving no living soul behind. But, he told himself, Neill had no dairy cattle, only stirks. The farm would survive untended for a day or two.

Munro recognised the strain showing in Keith's eyes. 'How do you see the sequence of events?' he asked. He knew that Keith's strength was his ability to see things clearly through another man's eyes, and that he would

113

be better using that ability than worrying himself sick over what might or might not be.

Keith pulled his mind back from the horrors. 'Something like this,' he said. 'They had it all pre-planned and they'd done their groundwork. During the night, or around dawn, there's a knock on the farmhouse door. When it's opened, men burst in and hold guns on the family. "If you don't do as you're told," they say to Neill, "we'll do awful things to your wife and daughter. And the first thing you do is to rearrange your straw bales to make a hollow rectangle of such-and-such a size." "I don't have enough bales," Neill says. "That's OK," he's told. "Joe Donaldson, next door, has already sold you his surplus and you've got use of his fork-lift. Fetch as many as needed. You've got until midday, or somebody dies." We must have crossed with his last load.

'Meantime, Pig Skinner has been talking with people or listening to gossip. At the last minute, he hears that the destination's been changed. Are they going to abort the job? Not yet. Somebody has the bright idea of phoning me and pretending to be the driver. Either I blurt out the new address, which I don't, or I lead them to it, which I'm fool enough to do. The operation goes ahead. The load arrives and . . . you know as well as I do, or better, what happened at the factory.

'The artic. leaves the industrial estate by the back way and comes down the Oldbury Farm Road where it's well-screened by the trees, and waits near the mouth until it gets the signal that the road's clear. You know fine how that road goes quiet at times. When there's a lull in the traffic, it crosses the road and goes down the dip to the farm and backs its trailer into the hollow between the bales. Neill boxes it in while the cab goes off to be hidden and later dumped in the carrier's yard.'

114

Munro had been nodding throughout Keith's explanation, but now he frowned. 'Why would they get rid of the cab?' he asked. 'They'd be needing it again, surely?'

'A point,' Keith admitted. 'But remember, if we're right, they were expecting to lead you away with a decoy vehicle and be on the road again within a few hours at the most. They wouldn't dare use the same combination. The plan would be for a tarpaulin or a new coat of paint over the trailer, and I'll bet there's a different cab somewhere, waiting for a phone-call to come in and collect the trailer when the coast's clear.'

'You make it sound plausible enough,' Munro said. 'Maybe it could have happened that way. But did it? That's what we still don't know.'

Ronnie had been waiting for his turn to speak. 'Aye, we do,' he said. 'There's still no sign of the McLellands, but there's two men keeping watch at the farm. 'You're a good guesser,' he told Keith.

'I wish I was as good with the horses,' Keith said. 'Where are they?' Gently but firmly he took the telescope away from Ronnie. Munro raised the binoculars again.

'One fellow's in the Dutch barn,' Ronnie said. 'He's watching the front of the house and the approach. He's in deep shadow, but you can just make him out when he moves. The other's at the back, tucked into the hedge just to the right of the dead tree.'

'I see the one in the hedge,' Keith said. 'Flat cap and a Mexican moustache.'

'Give me the telescope a wee minute,' Munro said. 'I can't make out a damn thing with these glasses.'

Keith handed over the telescope. 'If it's descriptions you're after,' he said, 'the one in the hedge is bald. He mopped his head just now.'

A silence fell as Keith and Superintendent Munro

115

studied the scene. Ronnie, unable to see any detail with the naked eye, grew restless. 'When do we go in?' he asked.

'Tonight,' Keith said.

'Tonight?' Munro echoed. 'Man, you can never be ready by then.'

'We must,' Keith said simply. 'The devil of it is that the nights are so short, which also means that dark's a long time off. If I could think of a way to make it in daylight, I'd go in sooner. You see, we daren't leave it a minute longer than we have to, for two reasons. Firstly, the signs are that they won't leave anyone alive when they pull out. And they'll pull out as soon as the road-blocks go. Could you persuade Doig to keep them at least until morning?'

'He'll not be keen,' Munro said, still scanning through the telescope. 'They're tying up two cars and at least ten or twelve men in shifts; including about six of the men who are trained in firearms, and they're few enough. You could persuade him yourself, better, with an anonymous tip that the load's going out by road tonight.'

'What's the other reason?' Ronnie asked Keith.

'The other reason is Deborah. She's been reared among guns. You should have seen her strip a Browning for Eddie Adoni. And she can shoot, too.'

'That wee lassie?' said Munro.

'Of course. She's followed me around like a puppy ever since she could toddle. Anything I did, she wanted to do. Well, I don't believe that any knowledge is ever wasted; so if I let her do something at all I'd teach her to do it as well as she was capable of. So I know she can shoot. She knows she can shoot. If one of those men puts down a pistol within her reach, she's quite capable of lifting it and saying "Stick 'em up", or whatever they say for it on

116

the telly these days. But those men don't know that she can shoot, and they won't believe it.'

Munro pursed his lips. Deborah could trigger a bloodbath. So also could any of the men now working for Chief Superintendent Doig, just by arriving at the farm, but he had more discretion than to point this out. 'What can you do that the S.A.S. cannot?' he asked.

'We may not have their technical resources,' Keith said, 'but we do have our skills. Ronnie's been a stalker all his life and he can move like a shadow when he wants to. We know every inch of the ground. If the worst comes to the worst, we can shoot. Most important of all, we have a first priority of keeping the hostages alive. Nothing else matters.'

'Right,' Ronnie said.

Munro put down the telescope. 'I do not believe that I am hearing this,' he said, 'and yet I know that it is so. Well, if it must be – and I suppose that this is also true – then, because I brought this upon your heads, let me give you some advice.'

'I'd be grateful,' Keith said. 'But . . . hold your horses. Somebody's come out of the farmhouse. I think . . . Yes, it's midday: it's the changing of the guard.'

Through the lenses, they saw a youth with long hair emerge from the Dutch barn and be relieved by a tubby man with spectacles. The man in the hedge was replaced by a taller man with protruding ears. The door closed again and all seemed deserted. Munro wrote down every detail that they could remember between them.

'Joyce's Boys, each of them,' Munro said. 'Now I can give Sandy Doig a report which will make my record shine in the dark.'

'You'll have a lot more to tell him by the time I say you can speak,' Keith said. 'Go ahead with the advice.'

117

'Surely.' Munro handed the telescope back to Ronnie. 'That is a fine glass,' he said. 'I could almost count the hairs in the man's ears. Well, now. First of all, try not to shoot anybody. Indeed, try not to kill or injure any one of them, but if you must do so, try not to do it with a gun. The law dislikes firearms.'

'Don't I know it,' Keith said.

'Next, if you should tackle one of them without shooting him, but he dies because you've been too rough, tie him up anyway. It will be good evidence that you did not mean to kill him and did not know that you had done so.

'Then, if you must shoot, shoot indoors. One of those men indoors is an intruder; outdoors, the burden of proof would be on yourselves. By the same token, shoot your man from the front, never from the back; you could never justify shooting a man to prevent his escape.

'Lastly, if you must shoot, shoot to kill.'

'*What*?' Keith was surprised into saying. 'You're sure you've got that right?'

'It is perfectly sensible advice,' Munro insisted. 'Think about it. Once you have pulled the trigger, the law will be concerned; it will not be greatly more concerned if the bullet finds his brain instead of his backside. In the circumstances, you may have trouble but in the end you will be exonerated. That is with the criminal side of the law. On the civil side, it is different. If you wound a man, he can sue you; and, the law's view of firearms being what it is, with every chance of success. Dead, he cannot sue you.'

'His family could,' Keith said.

'For loss of support, out of the earnings of crime? I do not think that they would get very far. Forbye, the death of such a man would save the taxpayer the cost of a trial

118

and of many years board and lodging, and I am myself a taxpayer. You'll remember my words?'

'To my dying day,' Keith said. He had known Munro for ten years or more, and now when for the first time he felt that he was meeting the real man he liked him better. 'But for now, would you mind spending some of the day keeping watch? We need to know how many men can be seen and the routine and times when they change over.'

'Surely,' Munro said. 'It will look well in my report, when you let me make one.'

Keith had become accustomed to the fact that the flat over the shop, where he and Molly had begun their married life, was now occupied by Wal and Janet and was decorated and furnished accordingly. But with his mind filled with worry and plans, he had forgotten again, so that when he rushed in through the flat door he suffered a moment of disorientation. Janet and Molly were sitting in tense silence, talked out. Molly looked up with frantic eyes as he came in.

'Nearly there,' he said as cheerfully as he could. 'We know where she is. I'll tell you when you need to know. We'll get her out tonight.'

'How?'

'I don't know yet. I'll think of something. Don't I always? First, I need your help.'

'Anything,' Molly said and Janet echoed her.

Keith and Molly each knew the importance of keeping the other busy during times of crisis. He took a second or two to regather his thoughts. 'Get on the phone,' he said. 'By this evening, I want a good rifle with integral silencer and flash eliminator, fitted with a Phillips night-sight – the Dutch-made one – and already zeroed. And I'll want to know what range it was zeroed at. And fifty rounds of ammunition, mercury-filled if possible. You may have to go as far afield as O'Neill in Maidstone. He can put it on a one-two-five train from London in the hand of a messenger, and you can get somebody with a fast car to meet it at Berwick-on-Tweed.'

'Are you going to shoot somebody?' Molly asked. She did not sound hostile to the idea.

'I don't think so,' Keith said. 'But if I'm fumbling around in the dark, I want to be covered by somebody with a rifle and a night-sight, just in case somebody else is watching me through one. When you've fixed all that, borrow Wal's car, belt out to Briesland House and bring back the metal step-ladder.'

'Anything I can do?' Janet asked.

Keith remembered what had been at the forefront of his mind when he entered the flat. 'You're the one who can do voices,' he said. 'Find another phone – the shop one, if you can't be overheard – and make an anonymous call to the police. Be Cockney. You're the disenchanted girlfriend of one of the gang. Mention Joyce's Boys. Say that there's a plan for getting the guns out the moment the road-blocks are removed.

'Then see if you can get hold of Paul York. He's putting up at the hotel. I'd like him to meet me here, threeish.

'After that, hang on and take messages. Ronnie's having a look-around and he'll be coming here. Tell him to wait for me. I've got Munro's car and I'm going out to find Sir Peter. I'll be back in an hour to an hour and a half. And,' Keith added on an afterthought, 'I'll be hungry.'

TEN

He returned in a little over the hour. Ronnie, grubby but pleased with himself, was already at the flat, and, with a drink in his big fist, was telling Molly and Janet the story of their journey up the hill insofar as he understood it. He had already mentioned Lairy Farm, but Keith was pleased to note that Molly showed no signs of rushing off in that direction.

'Somebody phoned up,' Janet said. 'He sounded too English to be true. He said that he represented the real owner of the guns, and he'd pay well for advance information when they turn up.'

'You may get more like that,' Keith said. 'And reporters, real and spurious. Give them all an evasive answer.'

'You mean –?'

'Yes.' Keith's idea of an evasive answer was well known.

Keith spared a few minutes to put flesh on the bare bones of the story which Ronnie had been telling, while Janet put food on the table. Then, between mouthfuls, Ronnie made his report.

'Those lads may be well-drilled for the city streets,' Ronnie said, 'but outside of the city they've just no idea.

121

They think that because they can see for a mile they can see everything in it. I went up the ditch between the kale and the stubble and then I was in dead ground. That damn covey of grey partridges that hatched by the midden was in front of me. I tried to keep them moving gently. If they'd been redlegs I could've done it but, being greys, they sprang of a sudden. Well, to a watcher, that might only have meant a fox. But when some pigeon came over and jinked when they saw me, they should have known there was somebody there. I was expecting a man with a pistol any minute, so I got behind a whin-bush and made ready to jump him if I had to. But not a bit of notice did they take. Silly sods!

'The dead ground got me to the corner of the stack of straw bales, and by then I was out of sight of the beggar in the barn. Those bales are too tight together to get between, but I could see in and there's a trailer in there right enough. So we've found the guns.'

'Never mind the guns,' Molly said in agony. 'Tell me about Deborah. Before you came in, Keith, he was saying that he'd heard Deborah's voice.'

'Don't rush him,' Keith said. 'I want to know the details.'

Ronnie nodded and went on. 'Neill McLelland has his tractor and his fork-lift parked between the gable and the stack of bales, so I tucked myself between them and was wondering what the hell to do next when I heard Deborah's voice. They were in the bathroom. The window's round the back, but there's a ventilator fan in the back wall. I heard Mrs McLelland's voice, too, and a man telling them to hurry up and get back next door. Deborah was needing to do a widdle, and Mrs McLelland had gone with her to help her with her things.'

'She doesn't need help any more,' Molly said indignantly.

This maternal pride was so ill-timed that Keith, whose feelings needed a safety-valve, gave a hoot of laughter. After a moment the others joined in, Molly with them.

Sir Peter Hay chose that moment to poke his shaggy head round the door. His equally shaggy eyebrows went up.

'Come in, Peter,' Keith said. 'Come and join us. And don't think us mad, laughing at a time like this. We needed to blow off steam. Have you eaten?'

'Thanks to you, no. I've spent what would usually be my lunchtime hunting through the estate office.'

'You got it?'

'I did. My memory was, for once, correct.' Sir Peter joined them at the table. He pulled out a folded plan and began to open it. 'I sold Lairy Farm about ten years ago, to tidy my boundaries. But when the alterations went ahead, a plan was filed with me, quite unnecessarily. I think the architect thought that I was still superior of the feu or else a conterminous proprietor. We still had it on file. Ah, thank you, my dear,' he added, as Janet put a plate in front of him.

'If anybody else turns up,' Janet said, 'they're out of luck.'

While Sir Peter tried to find words of cheer for Molly, Keith made a space on Janet's table and spread the plan of Lairy Farm between himself and Ronnie. He found the bathroom. 'Here?'

Ronnie squinted at the plan, muttering. 'Looks right,' he said.

'That would make sense. The big bedroom given over to the hostages, with the bathroom next door. One man on a chair in the passage could guard the lot of them.

123

You couldn't see whether the windows were boarded up?'

'Not from where I was. When I go back to collect Munro, I'll see if I can't pull in somewhere and take a look through the faur-keeker.'

'Telescope,' Molly said sternly. 'Don't you go teaching your niece to talk like that.'

Keith was still looking down at the plan. 'Ronnie,' he said, 'will you draw every damn thing you can remember. The positions of fences and hedges, the straw bales, the tractor and so on. We don't want somebody walking into them in the dark.'

'I'm not much of a hand at the drawing,' Ronnie said anxiously.

'Do the best you can.' Keith shifted his eyes to a different drawing and swore softly. 'Hot damn! Those two rooms are in the flat-roofed bit. I hadn't realised.'

Ronnie looked up from his attempt to draw a plan view of a tractor and withdrew his tongue from between his teeth. 'That bit was the old dairy,' he said. 'I mind that when they came to extend the house the roof of that bit was just hanging, so they put a flat roof on instead.'

'Does it matter?' Molly asked.

'I don't know yet. The windows will be sealed unless those men are daft – which, in spite of what Ronnie says, they're not. And the walls are stone. People forget about roofs, but what's been put up a piece at a time can be taken down the same way. I was hoping to get onto the roof, lift a few pantiles and cut through the battens under cover of the noise of a helicopter or something. But a flat roof's all nailed together and the nails are probably rusted into place by now.'

'Can't you get her out, then?' Molly was near tears.

'Yes, of course I can.' Keith sounded surprised that

124

anybody, especially Molly, could doubt his capacity for miracles. 'I don't know how yet. But to every problem there's a best solution and it's just a matter of thinking of it beforehand instead of afterwards. Peter, can you manage the other things I asked for?'

'No special problems. A tractor and trailer will be waiting behind the industrial estate from ten p.m., with a load of small straw bales, nothing over a hundredweight. Fold Farm will be deserted this evening. For noise-makers, I couldn't manage a helicopter but a light plane will be standing by and I've hired a low loader with two earth-movers aboard, to climb the hill whenever you say.'

'Well done,' Keith said. 'Just send me the bills as they come in.'

'My dear boy, just consider it my contribution towards my god-daughter's salvation.'

The others were struggling to follow the reasons behind these exchanges. 'Why Fold Farm?' Molly asked.

'Because it's a long way away,' Keith said, 'and because it's much the same layout as Lairy. I want some rehearsals in daylight before we start moving around in the dark. It looks like being a clear night. No moon, and no mist or cloud to diffuse the town's lights. Just starlight, and that's not a lot of light. Peter, could you seek out at least twenty of your most willing men, foresters and farm workers? No weaklings, mind.'

Sir Peter nodded gravely. 'If I tell them that they're rescuing a kidnapped child there'll be no holding them back.'

'Great,' Keith said. 'But tell them nothing for now. We've seen what happens when word gets around of our doings. At knocking-off time, have each of them told that there's a late job on. Report in wellies or soft shoes, no tackets, at Fold Farm at eight.'

'Will do.' Sir Peter hesitated. 'Is that all you want from me?' he asked wistfully. Sir Peter, Keith knew, was bored by the role of wealthy landlord, to which he had been born, and hankered after an active part in the excitements which occasionally came Keith's way.

'Not by a mile,' Keith said. 'I want you up on the hill, just below the main road, with a rifle and a night-sight. You keep scanning the ground through the infra-red sight to make sure that nobody I don't know about arrives unexpectedly.'

'I thought Wal could do that,' Janet said.

Keith went on speaking to Sir Peter. 'And you watch specially for a bright red spot which means that somebody else is doing the same thing. And if you see it you start shooting quickly and straight, because the odds are that he's seen the bright spot of your sight. Janet, you were saying?'

'Nothing,' Janet said.

'You wanted Wal tucked well out of harm's way,' Keith said. 'I'll try not to put him in danger, or anybody else. But if you don't want him exposed to any risk at all, say so now and we'll drop him from the team.'

Janet shook her head. 'He'd never forgive me,' she said.

'Anyway, Wal's short of three fingers and Peter's far the better rifle shot.'

Ronnie, busily drawing shaky lines on the plan, had fallen behind the discussion. 'What's with the labourers and the straw bales?' he asked.

Keith sighed. It was torture to his quick mind to stop and explain. 'I'm hoping,' he said, 'to get Deborah and the McLellands out, quickly and cleanly. Once they're out and away, we can solve the problem of anyone else in

126

the farmhouse any way we want. Frankly, I don't give a damn whether we arrest them, leave them to scatter or kill the lot of them. But during the first stage, the last thing we want is for men with guns in their fists to come rushing out of the doors. By the grace of God, there's tarmac right up to the front door at Lairy and a paved path to the back, so men in wellies can move silently even carrying a straw bale each. Ten straw bales stacked against each door should buy us some time.'

'Clever,' Ronnie said. 'Could we not manage a steel plate between the door and the bales?'

'Anybody pulling open the door and shooting, as he thought, into the night would give himself a hell of a fright,' Keith said. 'But we couldn't handle heavy enough plate quietly. That's very good,' he added, looking at Ronnie's sketches.

'It's gey rough.'

'It tells us what we need to know.'

'What about the windows?' Molly asked.

'I was coming to that,' Keith said. 'I don't expect any surprises there, because if I know farmhouses the windows have been painted shut for years and it takes time and noise to come out through glass. But the men who brought the bales take up positions, one each side of every window. Each man has a pick-handle and also a shotgun slung on his back, muzzle downwards. If anyone with a gun comes out of a window they clobber him if they can, and if they can't they blow him in half. Do we have twenty medium-priced shotguns in stock, Janet? I'm not letting that mob loose with Purdeys or Perazzis.'

'We can manage,' Janet said. 'But aren't you taking an awful chance with the law?'

'Book them out to me personally,' Keith said, 'on sale-or-return. That way the business needn't suffer.

We'll need something to make a sling for each gun, and a few rounds of heavy shot per man.'

Sir Peter Hay had started to make notes on several lists, to Keith's pleasure. When the baronet turned his attention to organisation and logistics, nothing would be forgotten. 'Is that all you want the men for?' he asked.

Keith was still looking down at the drawing. 'We'll decide later, when we have a final plan complete with contingency alternatives and signals. For the moment, I think there may be one task for them before they move to the windows. Janet, can I count on you for one special job?'

'Why Janet?' Molly asked. 'Why not me?'

'Because you'll be passing signals. And because, in the same way that Deborah's growing up among guns, Janet grew up among farm machinery. None of us knows more about tractors and things . . . .'

Paul York arrived promptly at 3 p.m. Keith led him up to the flat.

The shop had been closed, with an apologetic notice on the door. Wallace had been elected to go and relieve Superintendent Munro. Armed with lists, Molly, Janet and Sir Peter had been sent to gather equipment and to set in motion the whole complex operation, all in utmost secrecy.

Only Ronnie remained. The three men sat round Janet's dining table. Ronnie was very quiet. It had been explained to him, forcibly and with threats, that he was present as a witness and for support in the event of anything rough developing and that he was to keep his ears and eyes open and his mouth firmly shut.

'The time may have come,' Keith said, 'for out-and-out co-operation.'

'I'm glad to hear it,' York said.

'It depends whether you're who I think you are.'

York blinked. 'You know who I am,' he said.

'I know who you say you are.' Keith produced the Le Mat revolver from under the table. It looked enormous. 'And if that's who you really are, you spend the night in the basement under the shop. Eddie's position in all this is too damn suspect.'

'All right, then. Who do you think I am?'

'I think you're a copper with a background in the martial arts, and that you were seconded from the Lothian and Borders fuzz to join Special Branch and go underground, all under a carefully faked cloud.'

Hitherto, Keith had been distracted by York's size and his balanced movements and had hardly noticed his face. Now he realised that it was round, bland and neutral, its expression in the eye of the beholder. It was not a face to invite either trust or suspicion and Keith stopped trying to read York's soul in it. Only by reading the faint stiffening in York's frame could Keith detect that the big man was disconcerted.

'Just what leads you to that extraordinary conclusion?' York asked slowly.

'By which you mean, who told me? Nobody said a word. But I've never met anybody who moved, as you do, with the precision of a well-lubricated machine, except for dancers and top men in karate, kendo, judo and similar arts. And I have my own source in the police. Your information generally overlapped with his, but sometimes you were ahead of him and sometimes behind. That suggested that your information wasn't coming from the uniformed branch.'

Paul York was silent for a few seconds. Then he shrugged. 'You win,' he said. 'I'm Special Branch. I'll

129

have to be more careful from now on.'

'I'd hate to hurt your feelings,' Keith said, 'but it could be that you have a source in Special Branch without being *in* it. If you're a member, no way would you be separated from your card. So let's have a keek at it.'

For the first time, York's face registered an expression, mild amusement. 'Rather than spend the night in your cellar,' he said, 'I'll indulge you.' He took off a shoe and removed a card from under the insole. This had been issued only a few months before. It carried York's photograph, and identified him as a chief inspector in Special Branch.

'So far so good,' Keith said. 'I take it that you thought Eddie Adoni might be up to something?'

'One load, two purchasers,' York said. 'The same source tipped us that he was looking for a minder, and for an inducement he recommended me for the job.'

'You let the robbery happen, and so the murders, just so that you could find out who the other clients were?'

'Christ, no! Eddie must have rumbled me early on, because he pulled the wool over my eyes from the start. We'd assumed that the switch would happen after you'd done your stuff, so that the eventual buyer would get sound merchandise. We forgot that terrorists aren't always so fussy and that Eddie, who's made some heavy losses in the last few years, was desperate enough about money to save your fees. My guess is that I was meant to die with the rest. But the lorry got away early and Eddie kept me talking. He seemed to be discussing a phony fire in your factory, after we'd brought the overhauled and converted guns out the night before and substituted junk. In fact, I see now that he'd got wind of the changed destination of the load and was trying to winkle it out of me without giving himself away. So he saved my life without meaning to. He's been pulled in now and making a poor job of answering some very difficult questions.'

'But he left you with egg on your face, which you're trying to remove by making your own contribution to the case.'

'You can put that to music,' York said, 'and sing it.'

Keith thought to himself that if policemen wouldn't dangle their chestnuts in the wrong places he would not be asked to pull them out of the fire, thereby adding himself to the numbers of those in trouble. But the comment seemed better left unspoken.

'How's your night vision?' he asked.

York raised his eyebrows. 'Very good. Well above average. What's that got to do with anything?'

'That was the big question,' Keith said. 'If you'd given the wrong answer, you'd have spent the night in the cellar wondering why it was wrong. How good are you at the martial arts?'

'I started as soon as I could toddle, and I've gone as high as I can go. They fly me out to the Orient to judge contests.'

'Could you take out an armed man in the dark?'

York stared at him. 'I could. Easier than you could peel a banana, all things being equal. Whether I would is a different question. If you know where the guns and the gang are, you've done your bit. Tell the police.'

'I would, but –'

For the first time, York showed emotion. 'You can't have taken in what I said. This gang's too dangerous for amateurs like you. Tell me where they are, and the matter's out of your hands.'

Keith decided that the time for putting Paul York in

131

his place had arrived. 'I'd agree with every word,' he said, 'except that, to stop me interfering, they've snatched my daughter. But I know where they are, and they don't know I know. I could tell the police, but I'm not content to trust my daughter's rescue to any group which does not have her safety as their first and only priority; and especially not to a group which is far from blameless in the matter of the original crime.'

'You're laying that at my door, are you?'

'I didn't say so. But if the cap fits, wear it. A lot of the blame belongs to Munro, our local super., who wouldn't believe me when I told him that the load was at risk. And you two are the only officers who've had the gall to come to me for help. Well, you'll get help. I can give you the guns, and Munro the gang. But you'll get help on my terms or you'll stay here until it's all over; and that'll look bloody good on your record.'

York took no offence at this blunt speech, but Janet's clock ticked half a minute away while he thought it over. 'Let's see whether your terms are too stiff,' he said at last. 'What do you want me to do?'

'They're holed up in a farmhouse,' Keith said, 'with the guns nearby. They're being watched now, and we'll soon have an idea of how many there are and at what intervals they're changing over their guards. They seem to be keeping two men outside, one at the back and one at the front, and the reliefs come out before the guards go in. So what I want to do, just before the change, is to take out the two men outside; and then take out the reliefs when they emerge.'

'But?' York said.

'This object,' Keith said, 'is my brother-in-law. He's a hard nut. So am I. He can move very quietly when he wants to. I can, too. His night vision is superlative. And here's the snag: mine's no more than average. I was reckoning that Ronnie would have to go after each man in turn, with me as a back-up; but that could be disastrous, if one of them managed to make a squawk. The alternative was a crossbow with a night-sight, which I could put together out of stock. But that means killing.'

'And you don't want to kill anyone?'

'Let's be quite clear about this,' Keith said. 'I don't give a fart about killing any of these scum. But I don't want to spend the rest of the year taking fuss and flapdoodle from the law. In fact, if I had to kill one or two sentries, I was going to kill the lot and use the farmer's tractor to bury them. But I can see that that wouldn't do. So a second man to deal with the sentries would be a godsend. Then, when all's done, you deliver the prisoners to Munro and take charge of the stolen guns. Are you on?'

'Oh, yes,' York said. 'If your plan is workable, I'm on. But let me give you a piece of advice.'

'I'm knee-deep in advice. Munro gave me a lot of it.'

'Mine can be contained in one word. Succeed. If you pull this off, you'll be too heroic a figure for the law to pick nits over your taking it into your own hands. But if you blow it you'll be the scapegoat.'

'I know it,' Keith said.

For York's benefit, he went over his plan in detail.

If York was impressed, he refused to show it. 'It's wild,' he said. 'But it may work. That's little or no skin off my nose. I'm acting under duress.'

ELEVEN

Dusk that evening progressed with the agonising slowness of a healing wound. Time and again Keith thought that the light was almost gone, only to find that there was yet another degree of darkness to which his eyes could adjust so that he could still see the faces around him, the trees beyond, the trailer which had brought the bales and the farm road running down towards where, invisible in its dip, Lairy Farm crouched beyond the town road. The lights of occasional traffic gave his night vision an occasional setback, feeding his impatience with illusion.

Now was the hardest hour. All day he had cocooned himself in urgent activity and talk, but now he had time to think of the dangers to come and of the unthinkable penalties of failure. It would be as bad for the others, he knew, and worse for Molly, but there was nothing he could do to help. He could only wait, and hope that his bowels would not betray his fears.

At long last the light was all but gone from the northern sky. Keith rapped on the side of the foresters' van, where Ronnie and York had been protecting their eyes from passing lights. Each was dressed in black and with a blackened face. He could barely make them out as they emerged, flitted across the road and were gone.

He settled down to wait again. Around him he could sense the presence of the foresters, but all was remarkably quiet. There was no traffic up on the main road; Munro was holding it back on pretext of a faked accident. Keith kept one eye on Sir Peter's position, but no signal showed.

Cyril Todd peered out from the darker shadows of the Dutch barn and scanned where he knew the courtyard must be. He had a torch but its use had been banned except in emergencies. Instead, he fingered the pistol in his belt and thought about what he would do if some fool dared to come poking around the farm. He wanted action, or sleep. He got both. Before he was aware of any presence, there was a whisper in the air behind him and a chop from a hardened and practised hand put him out cold. When he came to, some time later, his wrists and ankles were tied, his mouth was sealed with tape and he was quite unable to move his head for the agony in his neck. He was the bald man with the Mexican moustache whom they had first seen in the hedge.

Jim O'Donnell was the long-haired youth who had been in the Dutch barn. He wished that he were back in its comparative comfort now, but Joyce had ordained that places should be exchanged in the interests of fairness. The hedge was full of unexpected thorns, so he stood on the path. Who, after all, was there to see him? He was minding his own business and whiling away the time until his relief with daydreams of rape and torture when Ronnie rose silently from the grass beside him. O'Donnell was holding a comb with the intention of tidying his hair before re-entering the farmhouse. In the dark, the comb was easily mistaken for a pistol-barrel. Ronnie lacked York's finesse and he was disinclined to take chances. O'Donnell found himself flat on his back

135

with an appalling pain in his groin and a great weight centred on the knee in his solar plexus, while one big hand twisted his wrist to an angle that nature had never intended to be possible and another maintained a grip on his throat which slowly deprived him of a consciousness which was already a burden to him.

Keith saw the blink from a carefully shrouded torch. He closed his eyes and acknowledged the signal by blinking the van's sidelights. The luminous clock in the van read twenty to twelve. According to Munro and Wallace, the guards had changed again at four and at eight, so it was a safe bet that they would change again at midnight.

It was time to move closer. He passed the word and picked up his own burden – two short, metal ladders, lamps, a torch, a shotgun and a pick-handle. A long file of laden figures trudged quietly after him. They crossed the town road and walked on grass as far as the back of the Dutch barn where a clump of trees stood on a triangle of cropped grass. Keith, Janet and Wallace went on while the other men thankfully put down their heavy bales and sat on them.

Keith looked at his digital watch by its self-illumination. Ten to twelve. The diversion was timed for ten past the hour. If nobody had come out by then they would go ahead regardless, and God help them if the doors opened just as the men approached the house. Six men had been counted doing guard duty, but the woman might be inside and there might even be a man or men excused sentry-go. Two had been dealt with. Two more and the odds would be improved, from desperate to merely difficult and dangerous. While Wallace cut the strings which held the ladders together and silent, Keith set about fixing the lamps.

Two minutes into the new day and Keith was worrying in earnest. The doors of the house stayed shut. The time for changing the guard might have altered, or the reliefs might be waiting for the others to come in. But already he could hear the distant drone of the plane, and a deep rumble suggested that Munro had released the north-bound traffic on the main road.

But their luck held. Discipline, for once, was its own worst enemy. At three minutes after the hour the front and back doors opened, spilling light momentarily into the darkness.

Paul York waited in the barn, sitting on the bumper of the farmer's car to disguise his height. But Nigel Higmott, Cambridge graduate and the hardest man in the group, was not expecting trouble and felt more than capable of dealing with it if it arose. He was doubly wrong. Paul York rarely felt free to practise the less defensive moves in the martial arts and so, rather than waste an opportunity which might never recur, contrived a complex sequence of seven different thrusts and chops before Higmott's knees buckled.

Ronnie, on the other hand, saw no reason to vary a successful technique. Sol Dorney, the tubby man with spectacles, was in any case a talker rather than a fighter. Ronnie came out of a clump of rhubarb beside the path and began with his knee-to-the-groin gambit ('Just to take his mind off other things,' Ronnie explained later). And that, disappointingly, proved to be more than enough.

Keith picked up the blink of the two torches and relayed the signal. The noise of traffic was growing and the aircraft was nearer. Two crocodiles of men plodded cautiously into view, darker shapes against the dark night; but for the paleness of the straw, he could not have picked them out at all. The men had been well rehearsed and those with the best night vision had been appointed foremen. Keith darted from one corner to the other. The lines of light up the sides of the doors were disappearing.

The plane was almost overhead. On the main road, a file of traffic was beginning the climb, its noise dominated by the rumble of Sir Peter's low-loader.

Men began to gather at the gable. Janet climbed into the seat and they grunted softly as they put their shoulders to the heavy machine and turned it into position. Then, as they melted away to guard the windows, Ronnie's big form loomed out of the darkness.

There was no more time to spare. The low-loader was at its nearest point and, according to his instructions, the pilot of the plane was beginning to turn and climb. Keith could hardly hear himself think. The noise might awaken some or all of the enemy, but it should buy them a few seconds by covering the first sounds of the attack.

He shone his torch on the wall, the signal to go.

The three men slung their guns and prepared to mount the ladders.

As Janet switched on the ignition, the lamps taped to the forks came ablaze. She pressed the starter. The lamps dimmed and the engine turned over without firing. Janet switched off to rest the battery, and darkness returned for ten seconds. Then she tried again, and again the starter ground. Suddenly, the machine fired, the lights came back to full brightness. Janet raised the forks and jerked the big machine forward until it had a grip under the eaves of the flat roof. Then the big fork-lift was straining up and forward. The roof refused to give. Keith, on his ladder, put his whole being into willing the machine to win. Janet closed the throttle and jerked it open, and the whole roof groaned and grated, assumed a curve and

138

then came free of its fixings and rose in one piece, complete with its ceiling, as if it had been a door hinged to the gable of the house proper. The lights of the house went out.

As planned, Wallace found himself looking down into the empty bathroom and he concentrated on covering the door. Keith and Ronnie were over the bedroom. Keith's first impression was that the room stank from occupation by too many people for too long and with the window heavily boarded. In the big bed, four people were waking in fear. For a moment he thought that the room was otherwise empty, then a head moved immediately below him as a man who had been dozing in a chair against the wall stumbled sleepily to his feet. Dazed by the noise and the sudden light, he was staring at the group on the bed. He was holding a pistol which Keith thought was either the Remington 51 or the French MAB.

The shotgun was unnecessary, and its use would have told every enemy in the house where to look for trouble. Keith let it fall back on its sling, steadied himself with his stomach and right hand on the wall-head and with his left hand he swung the pick-handle as hard as he could. The blow pulped the man's left ear and he staggered but stayed on his feet. Keith swung again and caught him over the temple. The pistol jerked and landed on Mrs McLelland's patchwork quilt, but still the man would not go down.

The McLelland family seemed paralysed with fear and surprise, but Deborah kept her head. She rolled forward on the bed, picked up the pistol in the two-handed grip which her father had taught her, and took aim on the man's chest. Keith was shocked to see that half her face was covered with a blue and purple bruise.

Even at his best, Sean Baxter was not bright. Joyce retained him because he never knew fear and because his virility was inexhaustible; since her widowhood, she had been glad of a man about the house. A sudden awakening and two stunning blows to the head had scattered what wits he had. He could only perceive, through the thickening mists, that the Calder child was pointing his own shooter at him.

Deborah's face, and the disfiguring bruises which looked black in that cold light, had distracted Keith. Now, he found that his mind could not think at the speed of events. The man must be stopped, and if anyone had the right to shoot him it was surely Deborah; but he did not want her to carry the mark of the killer for all her days. A stumbling pace towards the bed had put the man on a line between himself and Deborah, so that Keith could not use his gun.

He saw Deborah brace herself to fire, and realised that the bullet might well pass through the man and continue towards himself. He ducked down behind the wall-head.

Wallace James, although beyond the bathroom partition, could see the action. 'Deborah,' he yelled, 'throw it to me.'

Deborah blinked against the light and then swung her arm, throwing the pistol in the general direction of the voice. It landed in the bathroom and fired, shattering the toilet bowl and spraying Wallace with water.

At the same moment Ronnie, from his safer angle, decided to fire, but as he raised his gun it proved unnecessary. The man's knees folded at last, he bounced on the end of the bed and rolled to the floor.

Time had become precious. The shot, and Wallace's shout, would have raised the alarm. Keith's mind went into gear again. Five men had been accounted for. Six had been seen. And there was the woman. There might be other men. While part of his mind did these fruitless sums, Keith already knew that they were back on one of his contingency plans.

He dropped his pick-handle into the room and rolled over the wall-head, the gun swinging awkwardly on his back. A nail tore at his clothing, then his feet came down on Mrs McLelland's dressing-table and it was a long step to the floor.

Deborah, in an unfamiliar nightie, threw herself into his arms. 'Who did that to your face?' he asked.

'The lady.'

'Don't say lady, say woman. Go up to Uncle Ronnie.'

As Deborah's chubby bottom vanished over the wall-head Keith jumped for the door. It was locked and the keyhole was empty. The key must be in the pocket of the unconscious man. In a farmhouse, a duplicate was unlikely. Good!

He turned back into the room. Little Jean McLelland was already vanishing over the wall-head in the wake of Deborah, and Mrs McLelland was preparing to climb onto her dressing-table. Neill, haggard-looking with the strain, paused to give Keith a quick pat on the shoulder.

'Any more hostages?' Keith asked.

'Not that we know of.'

'How many men?'

'We've only seen three and the woman.'

'Up you go,' Keith said. 'Wallace James will take you to safety.'

Inside the house, the rumble of traffic was felt rather than heard and the noise of the plane was fading rapidly away. Keith heard somebody try the door and then throw his weight against it. But the door was heavy — transferred, Keith guessed, from some greater house that

141

was being pulled down. He knew what to expect next. He recovered his pick-handle and tucked himself against the bed, just beyond the swing of the door. He nodded to Ronnie and even against the lights he could see the shotgun steady on the door.

'You're too late, my friend,' Keith said softly. Already, Wallace would be on his way with the hostages and Molly would have received the signal to fetch Superintendent Munro.

The sound of the shot was lost in the noise of the hammer-blow. The lock jumped half out of the woodwork. When the man outside put a shoulder to the door again, Keith began his swing; and as the door flew back and the man followed through, already lifting a heavy pistol, the pick-handle took him in the face. The lower jaw went and a tooth pattered against the wall.

Take six from an unknown number and you have another unknown number. Neither of the men on the floor showed signs of stirring. 'Am I clear?' Keith asked.

Ronnie lowered his head for a view along the passage. 'Nobody in sight,' he said.

Keith kicked the pistol under the bed, dropped his pick-handle, climbed onto the chest of drawers and rolled over the wall-head, the shotgun cradled carefully in his right arm. From the far end of the farmhouse came the sound of breaking glass, but others could deal with whatever was happening.

'You're due to go and relieve Paul York,' he told Ronnie.

It was time for a change of tactics. Keeping his eyes firmly on the gap between the wall and the roof, Keith felt in his pocket for a whistle. It was the loudest whistle in the shop, guaranteed to stop a bolting dog in its tracks and bring it trembling to heel. He blew a series of rapid blasts and heard a patter of running feet as the men guarding the windows pulled back. Immediately, light began to glow as torches came on and were placed on walls and hedges and on the ground, all shining towards the house. It had been Keith's view that a single shot could put out a floodlight but that a hundred torches would present an insoluble problem to a group of men firing against the light while themselves under fire. Molly had been to Edinburgh that afternoon and had cleared out several of the larger shops.

The fork-lift was still throbbing gently. It put a new thought into Keith's head and he decided to modify his plans. He explained to Janet and provided her with the ball of string which was in his pocket for no more reason than that he never went without it. He placed his torch at the base of the wall and stood guard, with as much patience as he could find, until she was safely established behind one of the tractor's big wheels.

Then and at last he was free to go and oversee the general position. He made his way round the back of the house, careful to keep behind the ring of torches and stumbling occasionally over the legs of a prone watcher. Prisoners were to be held in that end of the Dutch barn screened from the windows of the house. At the corner of the barn a tall figure loomed up. Paul York shone a torch on Keith's face and on his own blackened features.

'I've handed over the prisoners to your brother-in-law,' York said. 'I'm going to take charge of the trailer.'

'Hang on a minute,' Keith said. 'It won't vanish again, and I may need your help. How many are we holding here? Four?'

'Five. One man, a slob in black leather and jeans, chucked a chair out through a window. He was climbing very carefully through the broken glass when one of our

143

men collared him.'

'Uninjured?'

'Yes.'

'Not now,' came Ronnie's voice from the barn.

Keith and Paul York moved round the corner to where Ronnie's torch was illuminating a neat row of prisoners, each handcuffed and sitting against the wall. They were in various states of disrepair and their mouths were taped.

'Have you been roughing up prisoners?' York demanded. 'We'll have none of that. Nothing justifies it.'

'Aye, it does,' Ronnie said. 'You didna' see my niece, and her face black and swollen with the bruises.'

'He's right,' Keith said. He managed a surreptitious wink and hoped that York could see it in the poor light. 'The brutalising isn't done yet. If Munro isn't here before I have time on my hands, I'm going to start some castrating around here. First, does any of these men have a broken limb?'

'Not to say a limb. I could break one for you, though,' Ronnie said helpfully. 'Or I bust that one's wrist earlier.'

'Wrist will do. Untape his mouth, and if he won't tell us how many men were in there with Joyce we'll hang him up by that wrist until he changes his mind.'

But O'Donnell, when his mouth was freed, proved to be in no mood to invite further discomfort. There had been seven men, he said very quickly, plus Joyce.

'We've dealt with seven,' Keith said. 'Now I'm going in after Joyce. And if I get any nasty surprises, my friends will pull you like a wishbone. Do you want to change your story?'

O'Donnell shook his head dumbly.

'I'll winkle the old biddy out of there for you,' Ronnie said.

144

'No you won't,' Keith said. 'You're too impetuous. And she's mine. York, will you come and back me up?'

'You're getting out of line. Wait for Munro.'

'He'll turn it into a siege. That bitch gave my daughter a bash in the face and I'm going to take her myself.'

'That's not a reason for me to lay my head on the block beside yours,' York said.

'At least wait outside. If she's armed and quick, I may need rescuing. After all,' Keith said persuasively, 'I only brought you along because you said you could disarm somebody in the dark.'

York sighed. 'That far and no further,' he said. He added, to Ronnie, 'And no beating up prisoners while I'm away.'

'Give me your torch,' Keith said.

The shattered window was in the gable of the house furthest from the straw stack. Out of the darkness Keith raised his voice, amplified by a trumpet improvised from a sheet of flabby plastic. 'Joyce Henshaw,' he bellowed. 'This is Captain Jenkinson of the S.A.S. We have removed your hostages and taken all your men. You are on your own now. The house is surrounded. You have five minutes to come out with your hands up. After that time, we're coming in with stun grenades and tear gas, and we will be shooting.'

There was no reply and no sign of life. The night had gone silent. Keith led Paul York on an oblique course which brought them to the side of the gaping window. Listening hard, Keith could hear nothing. He reached high with his hand, switched on the torch and risked a peep over the sill. The McLelland's living room looked deserted. Its door was closed or nearly so. He switched the torch off quickly.

'I'm going in,' Keith whispered.

'What about the five minutes?'

'Fuck the five minutes. If she walks out, well and good. If not, I'm going to catch her before she expects us.'

'This is stupid.'

'The stupidity's all my own. Shut up and stand by.'

Gently, Keith removed the last shard of any size from the window. He and his gun made entry at a cost of only slight further damage to his clothes and person. Using the torch for a few seconds from floor level he could see under the furniture. Unless Joyce was clinging to the back of the settee, the room was empty. He crawled to the door and, using the muzzle of his gun, eased it slowly open.

The house was pitch dark but there was a small area of faint luminescence that puzzled him. As his eyes adjusted it seemed to grow brighter and to develop hard edges. He identified it at last as the glow from the torch which he had left beside the fork-lift, seen along the length of the passage and through the open door of the far bedroom.

Keith waited. Entering the room had been ordeal enough without extending the risks. All that he stood to lose was the calling of his bluff.

He was soon rewarded. A shadow slipped across the area of luminescence. Joyce was moving from room to room, looking out of windows to assess whether any escape-route had been left open.

The shadow appeared again. He adjusted his grip on the gun, in case the woman was armed and turning his way. But the shadow grew smaller and moved through the bedroom door. He could make out the shape of a dumpy figure in a skirt. It passed out of his sight. He began to crawl along the passage, slowly and softly.

The noise, when it came, was sudden and dramatic – a

146

groan, a croak like that of an old-fashioned bulb motor-horn, and then the drumming of heels. He got to his feet and advanced, trying switches as he went; but the lights of the house had been killed when the roof was lifted.

If he had not expected it, the sight which greeted him in the torchlight would have been surrealist. Before climbing up to look over the wall-head at the apparently unguarded area outside, Joyce had hitched up her skirt so that Keith was confronted by an expanse of pale blue Directoire knickers. Janet had waited until Joyce's head and shoulders were outside before pulling the string which led to the fork-lift's lever, thereby lowering the roof onto her back. The woman was half crushed, the drumming of her heels against the ceiling already weaker.

'Janet!' Keith called.

'Hoy?' came back faintly.

'This is the last of them. Lift the roof just enough to let her breathe.'

'Not until she drops that cannon. It looks just like the Taurus three-five-seven you used to show off with, drilling holes through anvils and things, and I'm not coming out of cover while she's still holding it .... OK, she's dropped it.'

Keith heard the beat of the engine change. The roof creaked. 'Enough?' Janet called.

'No,' the woman gasped.

'Ample,' Keith said. 'Drop it again if she does anything but stay put.'

He walked back along the passage looking into the rooms as he went. 'We've got the lot,' he told York. 'You can go and guard the guns. Tell everyone to stay alert until Munro turns up.'

147

'Right.'

Keith returned to Joyce. The two men were inert but still breathing. He placed his torch carefully on top of the wardrobe and recovered his pick-handle yet again. Then he wound his hand round the flex of the light-fitting and pulled it down. It would have inhibited his swing.

TWELVE

When Keith emerged at last from the farmhouse, through the window, he was in a mood of elation although he knew that reaction would follow. The scene was brighter. Three police cars were splashing light around the forecourt. Officers, whom Keith recognised as belonging to Munro's personal team, were trying to inject order into an intrinsically disordered throng.

Munro himself was almost dancing, ogrish in the weird light. It was several seconds before he realised that he had lapsed into Gaelic. He began again. 'You did it!' he cried. 'By the good Lord, you did it! And nobody dead?'

'I don't think so,' Keith said. 'Not a shot was fired by our side, so I'll tell our men to say nothing about shotguns. Can we get them out of sight?'

'Put them in the boot of my car. Well done! Oh, well done! And now I take over the prisoners?'

'You do. But Paul York takes charge of the guns.'

'He shares the blame and he shares the credit,' Munro said. 'That seems fair. Here he comes now.'

'There are three more inside,' Keith said. 'They're in the far bedroom. Two men unconscious on the floor, and the woman stuck through the ceiling.' That seemed to

Keith to be the shortest way to express the facts.

'The woman is –?'

'Go and see for yourself. Call to Janet James and she'll lift the roof for you.'

Superintendent Munro turned away without another word. That night, he could believe anything.

Paul York arrived, breathing heavily, and took Keith's shoulder in a crushing grip. The big man from Special Branch was far from his usual bland self. 'What the hell have you been up to?' he demanded.

'You know exactly what I've been up to,' Keith said. 'I've been saving my daughter from where your balls-up landed her. And if you break my collar-bone, I'll sue you.'

York kept his grip but let some of the pressure off. 'With the guns, man. The guns.'

Keith divined that they were speaking of the trailer-load. 'What about them?'

'You know bloody well what about them. There's a hole cut in the roof of the trailer. The guns and ammunition were all crated and neatly stacked, and now there's a damn great hole in the middle. I'd guess that nearly a quarter of the load's gone for a walk. What have you to say about that?'

For the moment, Keith's inclination to involve himself in the problems of others was at a low ebb. 'Not a lot,' he said.

'I bet you haven't.' York's grip tightened again. 'Now I see why you kept me hanging around while I should have been standing over those guns. You've pulled one of your fast ones again.'

'Let go of me,' Keith said. 'I've no intention of taking you on at your own game, but I can deliver a kick in the crotch as well as the next man.' York took his hand

150

away. 'That's better. The only fast one I've pulled is your chestnuts out of the fire where you dropped them. I've been too damn busy rescuing my wee girl to give a thought to those guns. The nearest I've ever been to them was when I walked past the stack of bales. The most likely explanation is that the gang partly unloaded them, intending to send them out in small batches. Take a look around, and if you can't find guns you should at least find some empty crates.'

York considered the idea and found it reasonable. 'The buggers!' he said. 'I'm going to borrow a couple of men off Munro to guard what's left, just in case you're still coming it, and then I'm going to beat the truth out of one of those scum.'

'You were the man who thought that unarmed prisoners were sacred,' Keith pointed out.

'I can change my mind.'

'They'll be on their way to hospital by now.'

'Then I'll interrogate them there until they're old and grey,' York said. 'Hey, Munro! I want to talk to you.' His bulk cruised away across the forecourt.

The scene was still changing. A sort of order was emerging. Munro had instructed that nobody was to leave the scene. But Wallace, after delivering Deborah and her mother to the hospital, had carried out Molly's thoughtful instructions and visited Briesland House to collect food and almost the entire contents of Keith's carefully hoarded cellar. A party was developing in the Dutch barn. The officers had no power to dampen it and, their seniors being engaged elsewhere, they began to join in the jubilation and to accept surreptitious tots of Keith's vodka or tins of his beer.

Janet and Wal were dispensing most of the hospitality

151

from the open back of Wal's estate car. Ronnie was in attendance, but more concerned with being served than serving. Keith joined them and grabbed a paper cup and a huge ham sandwich.

'Where's Peter?' he asked with his mouth full. 'Didn't he get the signal. It's not like him to miss out on a celebration.'

'I signalled him twice,' Janet said. 'He didn't acknowledge, so I decided that he'd either dozed off or gone straight home. He's beginning to feel his age. Give me another gin and tonic,' she added to Wallace.

Wallace obligingly poured her another and topped up the paper cups all round. 'He's not that old,' he said. 'He'd want to be in on the fun. Perhaps one of us ought to go up and look for him.'

Dawn was near, Keith was tired and the long uphill walk was unattractive. 'I think that the cops would consider it their business,' he said. 'I'll mention it. Some time soon. Who's cutting sandwiches?' He poured some more of his own best whisky.

One of Sir Peter's foremen arrived to collect another bottle of whisky and one of vodka. Keith asked him to spread thanks pending his own tour of gratitude.

'Och,' the man said, 'the boys were glad to help get the lassie back. But is it right that we're on overtime?'

'It is.'

'Until we get home?'

Keith would have liked to say that the blame lay with the police and not himself for keeping them out of their beds, but he could not bring himself to be so churlish. He agreed. The party in the barn became more boisterous.

'This is costing a packet,' he said to Wallace. 'How would it stand as a business expense?'

'Bring me the receipts and we'll see what V.A.T. we

152

can recover, or what you can deduct against tax,' Wallace said unhappily. 'I honestly don't see it as a fair charge against the business. If you want a personal contribution . . . .'

'Good Lord, no,' Keith said, laughing. 'You've done more than enough tonight. It was the before-tax thing that I was after. But I take it that if I pay the bills I keep any compensating rewards? I might be able to screw something out of Eddie Adoni's insurers.' He was careful not to sound optimistic.

'Well . . . .' Wallace said slowly.

'You can't have it both ways,' Keith said. 'If we share the expenses, we share the rewards. If not, not.'

Wallace exchanged a glance with Janet. Keith had conjured profit out of nowhere in the past and he might do it again, but with Eddie Adoni jailed for attempting to steal his own load, his insurers were unlikely to have paid out anything. 'You pay the bills,' he said suddenly, 'and keep any spin-offs. Deal?'

'Deal,' Keith said. He smiled quietly to himself in the darkness.

Paul York had materialised again out of the darkness. His attitude was aloof but hunger and tension defeated him. He joined the group, accepted a beer and began to wolf down a sandwich.

'Is it right what Keith was saying, that half the guns are missing?' Ronnie asked him.

'I don't think half,' York said. 'I suppose there's no harm talking about it. Assuming that the crates were similar in size, I'd judge that twenty-two have walked. Near enough a quarter of the load. And if I find that any of you lot were involved, I'll break each of you in half or smaller.'

'You could try,' Ronnie said. 'But we was concerned

153

more with getting my wee niece and the McLelland family out safely to be thinking about your damn guns at the time. Are Miss Butch's old guns safe?'

'I'm assuming so,' York said. 'They were at the back of the trailer where there's been no interference, and there are crates there of a different shape and size. I can't get a look at the markings without starting to unload. Getting back to the modern weapons, I've searched as best I can in the dark,' he told Keith. 'There's no sign of guns or empty crates around the house or outbuildings.'

'For what it's worth, I'll tell you what I think,' Janet said carefully. Her voice was beginning to slur with tiredness and alcohol. 'If Newton Lauder's seething with Russian spies, isn't–'

'As a matter of hard fact,' York broke in, 'the Russians seem to be the one group not represented.'

'You know what I mean,' Janet said testily. 'Foreign spies, then. Isn't it more likely that one of those groups has pulled something clever? We were as secretive as we could be, but anybody watching us yesterday must have seen that we were getting ready for something. If they kept watch from the high ground, they'd have seen us gathering in Oldbury Farm Road; and that'd have told them where we were heading. Then, when we went in, our ears were full of the noise of the aircraft and the traffic and the fork-lift. We mightn't have heard if somebody had brought a silenced cross-country load-carrier – an Argocat or suchlike – down to the other side of the straw bales.'

'If it was something like that,' Wallace said, 'you'll find cut fences when you look in daylight.'

'I hope you're wrong,' York said, 'but you've put your finger on just what I'm most afraid of. If the guns reach some subversive group, word is likely to get back. If the

154

group has British sympathy, I'll survive. But if the guns turn up in the hands of the I.R.A. or some modern equivalent of the Baader-Meinhof gang and get used in an anti-British act of terrorism, I'm a dead duck.'

'Don't howl before you're hurt,' Keith said. 'Sir Peter Hay would have seen any such thing through his night-sight, and his brief was to smack a bullet against the wall of the house if he saw anybody unexpected approaching.'

'That's a relief,' York said. He had looked as if he would never smile again, but now his still blackened face produced a beam of genuine warmth. 'I'm glad your daughter's safe.'

Keith was still trying to find a suitably manly and unemotional answer when they were interrupted. Sir Peter's voice could be heard approaching. He seemed to be brushing off an importunate constable, but so far from his usual authoritarian manner he was bleating like a lost lamb. Keith was both relieved and concerned to see no sign of the rifle.

'There you are,' he said, homing on the group around Wallace's car. 'I told that bobby to let Munro know that I'm among those present. I take it that we won the day?'

'We did,' Keith said. 'All the hostages are safe, the gang in custody and most of the guns recovered.'

'Splendid! No thanks to me, though. The damnedest thing happened. But first things first. Is that a whisky that I see before me? Thank you, my dear.'

Sir Peter drank, and seemed refreshed. Keith was making faces at him. Sir Peter nodded minutely to indicate that he was aware of the policemen listening from the shadows. He flicked his thumb in the direction of the hill, from which Keith gathered that the rifle was safely bestowed where no certificate-conscious officer

155

was likely to find it.

'What happened?' Keith asked.

'Damnedest thing,' Sir Peter said again. 'I tucked myself into the bushes just below the main road and started to keep watch. That night thing's damned good, by the way. Much better than the one I've got. You'll have to get me one of them. Anyway, I scanned the country and nothing seemed to be happening. I was just watching you two lads moving in to tackle the sentries when I heard a sound behind me. Before I could move, somebody put what felt like a gun-barrel against the back of my neck and said, "Keep still." '

Sir Peter paused and drank again. Paul York uttered a low groan.

'He reached over my shoulder and took the whatsit away. There was nothing I could do about it. Frankly, I was half expecting a bullet where I wouldn't know much about it. But no. I heard him sit down behind me, and any time I moved or tried to look round he said the same thing again. "Keep still." Or, to be more accurate, "Kip steel." First time he said it I thought he'd made a nervous mistake, a sort of Spoonerism, but he said it the same way each time.'

'That's all you heard him say?' York asked.

'That's the lot.'

'Foreign accent?'

'I'd say so. But ask me from where and I couldn't tell you, not on the basis of two words. Anyway, I sat there like a dolt, praying that there wasn't, as you feared, somebody out with a rifle and night-sight, or that this character wasn't going to sound the alarm or take a shot at you. But, again, no. After a bit I got some of my courage back. My box of sandwiches was open beside me, so I took one and he didn't seem to object. He even

156

had the nerve to reach past me and help himself. In fact, he shared my sandwiches with me. I daredn't complain. If I'd had a second mug, I'd have shared my coffee with him, just to keep on his good side.

'I saw the lights of the fork-lift come on and heard one very faint pistol-shot. Then, later, the ring of torches began to light up, and everything began to look as if it might be going more or less according to plan. And still we sat there. I remember he handed me a hip-flask over my shoulder and I took a swig. It was something with lime, vodka at a guess. Very warming on a cool night.'

'Vodka?' said York.

'Yes. Nothing in that, of course. Barman in the club was telling me that the Scots are drinking more vodka than whisky these days, because you can mix it with more flavours of soft drinks.

'I saw the police-cars arrive, and I was given the signal to come down. Couldn't acknowledge it, of course. Then, later still, I heard a car stop on the main road above me, heading downhill. I think I'd heard the same car, which was a bit of a rattle-trap, go up a few minutes before. My companion said "Kip steel" again and I heard him move. When I got up the nerve to look round he was already up the embankment – he must have shot up it like a monkey – and a second later a car door slammed. I tried to get up to the top in time to see his number, but it's more rock-wall than embankment and I found I couldn't get up it at all. I got my torch out and looked around.' Sir Peter lowered his voice. 'He'd left the rifle behind, but the cartridges were scattered in the grass.'

'That mercury-filled stuff costs a *bomb*,' Keith said.

'I picked it up, all but two or three rounds which I dare say will turn up in the daylight. And then I came on down,' Sir Peter finished simply.

THIRTEEN

The new day passed in a haze of exhaustion punctuated only by occasional snacks and by dozing whenever no policeman happened to be wanting yet another statement.

Deborah, Keith knew, was at home with Molly. She had been released by the hospital as being in good heart and, apart from the bruising, uninjured.

The others, one at a time, were allowed to depart. Just when Keith thought that he could go home, he was dragooned into staying on to check the guns against the invoices as they were unloaded at last into the factory, under a guard of armed policemen sufficient to have repelled a mass invasion. He refrained from mentioning stable doors, and soldiered on. When he was free at last, a siege of reporters, some probably real and others more probably spurious, was lying in wait. Several followed his taxi out to Briesland House. He gave each one of them his evasive answer.

His car, repaired to the stage of being usable, was waiting outside the front door.

The police had passed a message and Molly had a meal ready. Keith was almost too tired to eat. He forced some food down, then fell into bed and slept twelve hours away. It was another bright morning before he came downstairs, fit, happy and starving.

He found Munro in the kitchen, taking coffee with Molly. The superintendent, an habitually moody man, looked as near to contentment as Keith had ever seen him.

'How's the slipped disc today?' Keith asked in greeting.

'A miraculous recovery,' Munro said. 'Just miraculous.'

Keith kissed his wife on the cheek. He had been asleep when she arose. 'Where's Deborah?'

'I let her go along to the market-garden,' Molly said. 'She got there all right, because I phoned Mrs Thing. If we stop her going to and fro on her own we'll make her nervous. She was a bit shy about the bruising, but I told her not to say anything and they won't either. Was I right?' she finished anxiously.

Keith thought it over while he poured milk onto cereal. 'Absolutely right,' he said at last. 'There's nobody running around now with any reason to molest her. And what's the latest on everything?'

'Reporters everywhere,' Molly said. 'They were camped in the drive. Mr Munro sent them packing, but they're probably waiting at the road until he goes away.'

'It is to be expected,' Munro said. 'There has been no more than a formal statement and ten thousand rumours. They know that the gang has been taken, that there had been hostages who have been released safely and that we have recovered most of the guns. Your name has been whispered. So the media have the bones of a story and no details at all.'

'Just the circumstances to drive them frantic,' Keith said. 'We told our team to say nothing, but that's too much to hope for. One of them at least will sell the story to the papers. But we warned them all, several times and very seriously, that anyone mentioning shotguns would land himself in the shit along with the rest of us. Anyway, it makes a better story if our party was only armed with pick-handles.'

'That is true,' Munro said. 'My men have been told that anyone mentioning shotguns will take over the duty of speaking to the schools about road safety. If there is one thing that a grown man hates, it is standing up before a classroom of giggling girls,' he explained. 'Those guns are still in the boot of my car and they make me feel like an accessory to an offence, which I suppose is the case. I will unload them in the privacy of your garage before I leave and we will forget that I ever had them.'

'Had what?' Keith said.

'That's good. Of course, when the full story gets out, you will have the credit for capturing an armed and dangerous gang while yourselves unarmed. You will become some sort of folk hero.'

'Big deal,' Keith said, opening his boiled egg. He was uninterested in becoming any sort of folk hero except insofar as it might help to boost the firm's business. 'But what about yourself and Chief Inspector York? Are you redeemed? What's been Superintendent Doig's reaction?'

Munro settled his bony frame more comfortably in the kitchen chair and smirked. 'At first, he was put out. Naturally. No man likes to have his case solved behind his back. I explained your reasons for not wanting direct police interference and that you had only brought us into it at the last moment and in conditions of great secrecy.'

'That satisfied him?' Keith asked.

'Far from it. He was winding himself up to make an

official complaint when York suggested, without quite saying it aloud, that if it came to an inquiry Sandy Doig could be made to look a fool. Lord, but that man York is subtle and devious! That, I suppose, is how one gets into Special Branch. He made it clear that, if criticism is in the air, Sandy would be as vulnerable as anybody. But if, on the other hand, we formed a mutual admiration society, each, in his report, praising the zeal, intelligence and discretion of the others, it might well be overlooked that Sandy Doig had never asked the right people the right questions when the right answers were just awaiting the asker. So now we are agreed. The case has been solved on the basis of "information received", as are most cases; results have been obtained which are very satisfactory from all points of view, and everybody has what he wants.'

'Except for the missing guns,' Molly said.

'We are not saying too much about that,' Munro said in tones of mild reproof. 'Indeed, the press statement makes no mention of them at all. After all, in very few cases is one hundred per cent of the haul recovered.'

'There's always some wastage?' Keith suggested.

'The very word! As long as the other guns are not used in this or a friendly country, Chief Inspector York's reputation will remain almost as untarnished as my own,' Munro said complacently. 'The present indications are that the missing guns never reached Newton Lauder at all. Two Edinburgh men have been found who say that they stopped for a snack at the transport cafe at Logiemuir, at about the time when the vehicle would have been in that area. They saw a van parked beside a blue, articulated lorry and a man on the van's roof. They thought nothing of it at the time, but now it seems that the driver might have stopped for food and some opportunist thieves pulled their van in on the blind side of it and went in through the trailer's roof, rather than through the doors which were in full view.'

Keith kept his face carefully blank. 'And has nothing happened to suggest the opposite, that the load did reach Newton Lauder intact?'

'Nothing,' Munro said; and Keith, who had long experience of the superintendent as an adversary and occasionally as an ally, was sure that he was not dissembling. 'But York is still not quite content. I feel that the man is worried. Perhaps it is that opportunist thieves would not have the contacts for selling the guns abroad. Their outlet would be the criminal black market.'

Molly paused in the act of filling Keith's cup. 'But what about – ?' She broke off as Keith kicked her ankle.

Munro looked at her, smiling, with his eyebrows raised.

Molly faltered, blushed and recovered. 'I was just thinking,' she said. 'I think that he may be worrying himself needlessly. Coincidences do happen, but you'd have to be up the pole to believe in the coincidence of opportunist thieves robbing a lorry which another gang had already marked down. Couldn't it be that one set of agents was on the job already, the P.L.O. or somebody like that? They were following the lorry in a van or a big car and they took their chance when they saw it to get the arms they wanted for their own reasons. They only took twenty-two boxes because that was all that they could carry.'

'Or maybe Eddie Adoni had yet another customer,' Keith said.

'Either of you could be right,' Munro said, 'or the truth may be something else again. Perhaps we shall

162

never know. And now, if you've finished your breakfast, perhaps we can get those shotguns out of my boot and I can go on my way feeling like a responsible officer of the law once again.'

With twenty-three shotguns removed from the boot, Munro's car rode several inches higher on its springs.

Keith had intended to slip away but Molly almost dragged him into the house, sat him down and poured more coffee.

'I've already got coffee oozing out of my every orifice,' he complained.

'But I want to talk to you,' Molly said, 'and you only stay in one place when you've got a cup in your hand. Are you diddling Wallace again?'

'I never diddle Wallace,' Keith said indignantly. 'I just let him diddle himself sometimes. Has Wal been on the phone already?'

'Not Wal. Janet. She said you let Wallace choose whether the costs and the rewards belonged with the firm or with yourself. And she said that whenever you seem to be giving the sucker an even break he'd better count his fingers afterwards. Well, that's what she said. Because of Eddie Adoni being in jail and his insurers not paying out, Wal chose to stay out of the financial thing, but they're beginning to wonder whether they've been had. Have they, Keith?'

Keith sighed. He had hoped to postpone this discussion for several days, perhaps for ever. 'I'll tell you something,' he said. 'I think I can screw a reward out of the real owner of the guns, His Coffee-coloured Excellency. And I'm planning to share it with Wal and Janet anyway, because they backed us up so handsomely yesterday and last night. I couldn't have got Deborah back without their help. We owe them.'

Molly looked at him with suspicion. 'Then why didn't you say so last night?'

'Because I want it to be a gift, not a business deal.'

'Why do you want it that way?' Molly persisted. 'And don't tell me you're being noble and making a grand gesture, because that wouldn't be you.'

Keith muttered something about drops of water wearing away stones. 'All right,' he said. 'I'll tell you more. If, and only if, you'll promise to keep absolutely mum about it until I tell you.'

'I promise,' Molly said.

'Well, don't forget. If I'd told this to Wal and Janet last night, they'd have opted for a half-share of the costs and of all the rewards. But I think there's more to come. And I feel entitled to cut myself a piece of cake. Last night it was only a gut-feeling, but now I'm becoming more and more sure that those guns did reach Newton Lauder despite what those Edinburgh men told the police. And you said something to Munro which may have given me a useful hint.'

'You didn't let me say anything about the man who held up Sir Peter,' Molly said. 'Janet told me when she phoned.'

'Munro didn't know anything about that,' Keith said. 'Interesting, isn't it? Of course, York looks much better if it's thought that the guns were stolen at Logiemuir and not while he was just a few yards away. And York was present when the statements were taken. He knew that I didn't go beyond what I knew from my own knowledge – what Peter told us would have been hearsay. Peter was the last to make a statement – he spent most of the night seeing that the men all got home and that the tractor and things were all safely returned. So I think that York got hold of Peter and said that he'd be just as happy if that

164

part of the tale never came out. He's probably said the same to Ronnie and Wal, and I wouldn't be surprised if he gets hold of me during the day. But he never expected Janet to mention it to you.'

'And that's why you're sure the guns all got here?'

'That's not the only reason,' Keith said, getting up. 'Thanks for the coffee. I must go. See you later.'

'Keith, promise me that you won't do anything which might put Deborah into danger again!'

'I promise.'

'What was it I said that gave you the clue? You can't just –'

But the door had closed. Apparently, he could.

During that morning, the news leaked out that Deborah had been among the hostages and that Keith himself had led the rescue party. The immediate frenzy among the reporters hampered Keith's efforts to deal covertly with the host of details still requiring his attention. He was forced to make much use of the telephone in the flat above the shop. Despite her promise Molly must have dropped some hint, because Janet welcomed him without reservation.

One of his calls was to Mr Smithers at Millmont House. The deep, smooth voice sounded very pleased with life in general. 'Mr Calder? I thought that I might be hearing from you.'

'And you were right,' Keith said. 'I think that we should meet.'

'I was about to suggest it. Would you like to dine with me here?'

'I would very much. But my wife has always preferred me not to visit Millmont House.'

'I can understand that,' Mr Smithers said. (Millmont

House, about twenty miles from Newton Lauder, func-
tioned as if it were no more than a very up-market hotel,
club and health farm, but its speciality and *raison d'être*
was an in-house call-girl system unsurpassed in Europe.)
'The ladies here still speak highly of you.'

'I helped them once,' Keith said. 'No more than that.'

'Of course. Where, then?'

Keith was about to suggest some secluded rendezvous
when he remembered that there was nothing confidential
about his dealings with Mr Smithers. 'How about the
Newton Lauder Hotel at eight?' he suggested. 'The
cocktail bar.'

'Eight, then. I'll look forward to meeting you.' And Mr
Smithers disconnected.

Another call was to Molly. 'It looks as if I'll be late,' he
said. 'It's a busy day and I can't make any progress for
reporters.'

'I suppose,' Molly said. 'Try to give me warning and
I'll have a meal ready.'

'How's Deborah?'

'Concentrating too hard on living her usual life. She
hasn't said a single word about her . . . adventure. And
she's gone back to playing with her dolls. Wouldn't it be
better if she talked about it?'

'Probably,' Keith said. 'But don't try to draw her out,
let her make the choice.'

'All right. I wish we could get her interested in
something new.' Molly sounded worried and Keith
guessed that she was hiding a deep concern.

'Tell her she can come around with me for a few days,'
he said. 'That usually perks her up. Well, see you later.'

'Hold on,' Molly said quickly. 'Keith, what was it I
said which gave you an idea?'

'You always give me ideas.'

166

'Seriously, Keith.'

'Seriously, only three words. I doubt if you'd remember any of them.'

In mid-afternoon an erroneous rumour that the police were about to make a full and crucial statement drew off his tail of reporters. The rumour was spread by friends in the rank and file of the local police at Keith's request, and Superintendent Munro proved to be in no great hurry to deny it. Keith was freed to start tying up his loose ends.

One of these brought him to his brother-in-law's home. He found Ronnie in the kitchen.

'Where's Butch?' Keith asked.

Ronnie had been dripping sweat into a pan of sausages but he abandoned the effort. 'If I knew that,' he said, 'd'you think I'd be wasting my time trying to remember how to cook? Come away ben and have a beer.' He dropped the charred mess into the sink and led Keith through into the living room which Janet and Molly had decorated and to which Butch had added her own touches. As a setting for the rough-hewn stalker it always seemed to Keith as appropriate as a lace frill round a manhole-cover. Ronnie hunted in a veneered cocktail cabinet and found tins of beer. 'I've not clapped eyes on her since the afternoon of the day before yesterday.'

This was what Keith had come to find out. 'That would be when you brought her up to date, the way I told her you would?'

'Aye. Now that her guns are here and she's got you to deal with them, maybe she's had all that she wants from me. It didn't seem that way but, with women, who can tell?'

'Amen,' Keith said. He shifted in his chair and wished

167

that Ronnie had been left to choose his own furnishings. Women, with their less weighty shoulders, can be comfortable in a chair that crucifies a man.

'Did they find all her guns in the trailer?' Ronnie asked.

'Her crates were all there and untouched. Butch came into the station last night and we opened them up for her.'

'It's a wonder she didn't come in by. I'll tell you this, Keith man, and don't you go telling Molly. I'm sair worried. There's been women have come and gone in my life, sometimes not much of a loss and sometimes a damned good riddance. But this one's special. Some of her clothes is still here, but I'm awful feared that some day I'll come home and find they're gone. If it's all done, surely the least she could do is to tell me?'

Keith had never seen his rough-hewn brother-in-law so close to tears. He was moved to pity. 'If it was over,' he said, 'she'd do that. Don't worry, she'll turn up. She's probably in work and sent you a message that you didn't get. Come out to us for a dram and a meal about this time tomorrow and if she's still adrift we'll sort it out. Good God, after getting Deborah and a couple of tons of small-arms and ammunition back from an armed gang, one small, Polish ballerina shouldn't be much of a problem. Did you have a chance to look round Lairy Farm in daylight?'

Their conversation moved away from the disquieting absence of Butch although Keith could tell that Ronnie's thoughts were still with the missing dancer.

From Ronnie's home, Keith headed eastward out of the town and then turned south. He passed Deer Hill and entered an area that was off his usual track. He tried

168

several casts along narrow, half-forgotten roads that laced the farmland, going almost nowhere. The telephone directory had given him a clue. He could have telephoned to ask for directions, but between innate discretion and over-confidence in his sense of direction, he had not.

He found it at last, and it was just as he had thought he remembered. A sign-board, once bright with primary colours but now dulled with age and almost lost in a sprouting hedge. It said 'Springbrae Stables', and underneath in smaller lettering, 'Prop: J.Batory'.

'Ha!' Keith said. He swung in through the gateway.

Ponies and horses were grazing lazily in two large paddocks shaded and sheltered by established woodland. The stable-block and the house seemed deserted but, from a small cottage which seemed to have been dropped behind the stables as an afterthought or by accident, a middle-aged woman in jodhpurs emerged in response to a toot on his horn. They met at the corner of one of the paddocks.

'Hullo,' Keith said. He invested the word with all the warmth he could project.

'Good evening.' The lady seemed unimpressed. Her voice was Anglicised Scots and peevish. 'Did you want something?'

'I wanted to ask about riding lessons for my daughter.'

The woman pulled a crumpled broadsheet out of her hip pocket and pushed it at him. 'This will tell you our terms. But as for making an appointment, you'll have to speak to Mr Batory. The phone number's on the letterhead.'

'Your charges seem reasonable,' Keith said. He decided to probe a little further. 'Couldn't you look in the book and make an appointment for me?'

'No, I could not,' she snapped. 'I'm supposed to be the secretary as well as the stable-person and general gopher. But nobody tells me what's going on around here any more. I can't help you.' She clamped her lips shut in a vicious little line.

She was helping him more than she knew.

'Where would I find Mr Batory just now?' Keith asked.

'I'm not his keeper.'

'Of course not. But I'm going away for a few days and my wife hates being left to make arrangements.'

She hesitated, but feminist sympathies won the day. The man must never be hindered from shouldering his proper burdens. 'He spends most evenings in the Polish Club in Newton Lauder,' she said reluctantly.

'In Bank Street?'

'I expect so. If you see him, you might ask whether we're opening for business tomorrow. It would be nice to know.'

Keith looked around. He was seeing the sunshine today, it seemed, for the first time. 'It's a lovely place,' he said. 'Your horses look well-kept. You've just the fourteen?'

'That's the lot. And poor old Caesar – the big roan – he's been lame for the last fortnight. We'll get by for now, but if Caesar isn't fit by the start of hunting proper we'll be short.'

Keith drove away grinning.

FOURTEEN

Keith knew where to find the Polish Club. A former lady-friend had lived nearby and he had noticed the plate without paying it any attention. He parked some distance away, in case some prowling reporter should recognise his car, and walked.

The club occupied what had once been two flats at the top of a mellowed, stone-built tenement block. The door was between two shops. Keith paused on the threshold. He wondered whether he was ready for any kind of confrontation. His thoughts were only beginning to come together. Yet he could make no more progress without asking questions, and time might only scatter the loose threads to where he could never catch them up again. He took a deep breath and went in.

The severe but well-kept stair climbed past flats labelled Kubicki and Tobiczyk. Evidently the block had become a Polish enclave. At the top was a single door, its blue paint almost concealed by notices insisting that the club was private, that non-members were never admitted and that those wishing to join should seek an appointment by telephone.

He tried the door. It was stiff but unlocked. The club's management must have felt that the inhospitable notices were protection enough.

As he climbed, Keith had been aware of a rhythmic vibration which pulsed through the fabric of the building. From the landing, he could hear faint music; but as he entered the club the volume rose and he could hear voices and make out the tapping of many feet. He followed the noise to another door and pushed it open, to be met by tobacco-smoke, a blast of heat and noise and the smell of mixed alcohols.

He had found the main clubroom, two rooms thrown together but still too small for the crowd of about twenty men, most of them elderly, who were packed sociably inside. There was a small bar, squeezed into a corner like a stranger at a feast.

Four of the tables had been pushed together in the middle of the room and on this precarious stage, her head dangerously near the ceiling, was Butch. She was the only woman in the room and Keith thought that she was very conscious of it. She wore a costume which Keith half recognised, half guessed to be Polish and she was dancing. Her dance might also have been Polish and traditional, but he thought that she was improvising within the framework of a traditional style. The dance expressed triumph and yet there was sadness to be seen in it. Butch was an artist.

She was the first to see Keith. She froze. The stamping of feet died slowly away. Only the music throbbed on until somebody stopped the tape. Through the silence, Keith heard whispers and his own name. He had time to recognise several customers of the shop and the saddler who stitched old gun-cases for him.

'I knocked and knocked,' Keith said, 'but I couldn't make myself heard above the music.'

A room full of men can never be quite silent and yet its

172

silence can seem much deeper than that of an empty room. Keith could hear the beat of his own heart and the hiss of the blood in his ears. Then Butch stooped to put a hand on the shoulder of the nearest man and jumped lightly down from the table. She squeezed her way towards Keith. She was smiling, but with an effort.

'The wean,' she said. 'How is she, after her bad time?'

'Bruised,' Keith said. 'Nothing worse.'

'Is good. I prayed for her.'

Keith felt uncomfortable. He had not thought to try prayer. 'We want to take her mind off it,' he said. 'I came to ask whether you'd give her dancing lessons.'

'Happily,' she said. 'Any time.'

The question and answer – unexpected even by Keith, who had been impressed by the excellence of the idea even as he heard himself uttering it – seemed about to relax the tension in the room. But a stocky man in his fifties, with the kind of knobbly and high-cheekboned face which Keith thought of vaguely as being Baltic or Slav, had risen and pushed his way to Butch's elbow. He was gripping an old revolver without seeming quite sure what to do with it. Keith took several seconds to recognise it.

The feeling in the room was hostile again. Keith realised that they were waiting for him to speak. He also realised that he might have put his head into the mouth of a very unpredictable lion. His own mouth was dry.

Say something irrelevant, he told himself, while they settle down. 'I wouldn't use that thing if I were you,' he said. His voice seemed to have gone up in pitch. 'It must be as old as you are and they never were much good anyway. On the other hand, the Radom factory never made many of them before they switched to a version of the Browning. A collector of early revolvers would

173

probably pay over a hundred quid for that one, which would buy you something more serviceable.'

The man said a few words in what Keith assumed was Polish and gestured with the muzzle of his revolver. There were a few nods but also murmurs of disquiet.

Butch, who was indisputably their leader, silenced him with a word. For Keith's benefit she switched to her own quaint pidgin-Scottish. 'Do not be fiel, Jan,' she said. 'If he knew nothing, you tell him muckle by showing that thing. If he knew muckle before he come, Mr Calder is too canny to come without telling his friends.' Jan would have spoken again but she rode him down. 'Enough,' she snapped. 'Sit down. You also sit,' she told Keith. 'Sit and drink and talk.' And she rounded on a small man near the door. 'Why was door not locked? You go and fix.'

Somebody moved to a bench to free a chair for Keith. Jan resumed his seat at the square of tables and laid the revolver in front of him. Butch took the only armchair, which seemed to have been brought from somebody's parlour to act as a throne. In this company, she was a queen. 'Now,' she said, 'tell us why you come.'

'I wanted to see you,' Keith said. 'And I wanted to find Mr Batory.'

Jan smiled grimly. 'You found me,' he said.

In for a penny, Keith thought, in for a pound. 'I know what you did two nights ago,' he said.

There was a brief sibilance as a dozen men drew breath together.

'When you find out this?' Butch asked.

'Let me put it this way,' Keith said. 'I could very easily have told the police before I came here, but I didn't. I don't need to tell any of you about what happened the night before last. I rescued my daughter

174

and that was the only thing which mattered. The capture of the criminals, the recovery of the guns, the fact that some of the guns have vanished, all those things were incidental. They still are.

'But when I had time to think, I guessed what had happened. And I came here tonight because we still have business to do and I like to know who I'm doing business with. So I want to know why.'

'Tell us how you know, and when,' Butch said.

'And then you'll tell me what I want to know?'

'Perhaps. First, you talk.'

'Very well,' Keith said. 'When the guns were recovered, eleven cases were missing from the middle of the trailer, through a hole in the roof. The police were given information suggesting that the smaller theft had happened before the load ever reached Newton Lauder. This, for me, doesn't ring true. No doubt the police would think the same. But because they can't believe that the guns could have been taken from the trailer while the rescue was going on, and in the presence of a Special Branch officer who desperately wanted them back, they're forced to act on the assumption that those witnesses were telling the truth. Can I take it that those witnesses were put up to it by yourselves?'

'No questions yet,' Butch said.

Somebody had put a drink in front of Keith and he took a sip. It tasted like bottled flames faintly flavoured with tonic water, but he scarcely noticed.

'I looked down from the main road,' he said. 'I saw what must have been the vehicle carrying the guns as it approached Newton Lauder. If there had been a hole in its roof, I'd have seen it. But I haven't told the police. Does that satisfy you?'

'Go on,' Butch said.

175

'Unlike the police, I was prepared to believe that the trailer could have been robbed again while my rescue was going on nearby. It was dark. Deliberately, we were making enough noise to have drowned a brass band. It could have been done. But it would have needed some prior organisation. How could whoever-it-was have known that I would create an opportunity for them in that time and place and manner? We had been as secretive as we possibly could so as not to endanger the hostages. Anybody watching us might have guessed that something was up; but by the time they could have known the details, it would have been too late.

'Then Molly said – '

'Molly is his wife,' Butch put in. The whole room was listening intently. The hostility was fading. Another drink appeared in front of him.

' – said something which reminded me that, because your antique guns were also on the lorry, I had told my wife's brother to keep you informed. He is a professional stalker and better at reading the signs than the police are. I asked him to look around the farm. The ground is very hard and dry. He could make out nothing in the stubbles, but in the grass he found some vague marks. None that he could swear weren't made by cattle, but they were very blurred. That made me think of horses with padded hooves and taped harnesses, perhaps given tranquillisers to reduce the risk of a sudden whinny, coming in across the farmland.

'So somebody knew our plans. Somebody Polish. And I remembered seeing a sign-board at the local stables with the proprietor's name on it. A Polish name. I also remembered that a contingent of Poles had been stationed near here during the war. After the war, none of them wanted to return to a Poland under Russian

176

domination and some of them settled in the neighbour-hood. Many of those were ex-cavalrymen.

'I have just counted your livestock, Mr Batory. Fourteen, including two Shetland ponies which would be too small for such a job, and the big roan which is lame. That leaves eleven. Twenty-two cases went missing. Two to a horse or pony – the logical way to load them.

'Then again, there's the hole in the roof of the trailer. It would have been easier and quieter to force the back doors, but that would only have exposed the antique guns, which had been loaded last. There would have been no point in your stealing the antiques which would come back to Miss Baczwynska anyway.

'And then, to dispel my last doubts if I had any, I come along here and find you in the middle of a celebration.

'You shouldn't have got away with it. If I may say so, you Poles are impetuous; and the plan must have been scrambled together in a hurry. Yet it seems to have gone smoothly, with one exception. You knew that I had sent a man with a rifle and night-sight up the hill, to keep watch in case of surprises. You had to neutralise him, so one of you crept up on him and held a gun, or what purported to be a gun, to his back.

'That fact should have alerted the police, and if they had investigated quickly with it in mind they would have found the marks in the grass. They would have found your horses resting after a night of hard work. But the only policeman who knew about the man on the hill was the Special Branch officer who had been on the spot. He would very much prefer that the guns had been taken before the lorry reached Newton Lauder. So he said nothing.'

Jan Batory grunted suddenly. 'You think you know it

all,' he said. 'But none of this is proof.'

'Of course not,' Keith said. 'And in a few days, all the small clues which might have furnished proof will have gone.'

'So what you want from us?' Batory asked. 'Money?'

'Not unless I earn it,' Keith said. 'I want to know more. I want to know why. At the moment I can only guess. I want to be sure. So that I know what to do.'

There was a murmur of concern in the room and then silence again. They waited. Even dressed as a peasant, Butch dominated the room. She decided.

'It can do no harm now,' she said. And she looked at Keith. 'Those guns are gone and can not be recovered. If I tell you why, maybe you will understand and help us.

'You hear of Solidarity?'

'The union? Yes, I know of it.'

'Why you smiling?' she demanded.

Keith wiped the smile off his face. He had offended. 'I was pleased that I'd guessed right,' he said.

'Was more than that. You think Solidarity is funny?'

'No,' Keith said. 'I think that Solidarity is far from funny. I think that it may be the beginning of one of the most important things happening today. But look at the background from our point of view. In this country we're cursed with unions whose top men mostly lean far to the left. Some of them are dedicated to ruining our economy, knowing that this will help the aims of communism. Their ideal would be to bring Britain under Russian rule. They see that as bringing the working man's Utopia. They close their eyes to the fact that you, in Poland, have the only real union behind the iron curtain, and it is a union which the Russians are trying very hard to stamp out. If anything amuses me, it is the contrast with our unions and the verbal somersaults which our union men

178

turn when they're trying to explain it away. Those are funny.'

Butch considered Keith's words and finally nodded. 'Is funny,' she agreed without trace of a smile. 'But in Poland is not funny. Polish peoples do not want to be communists or have Russian masters. Russians say, very loud, Polish peoples are free and more richer than peoples in west. But we know this is not true. Russians fix prices they pay for food and other things they buy from Poland. So Russians get cheap food and goods. So Polish peoples is kept poor.'

'And so ... Solidarity,' Keith said.

'Aye, so. But when Communist Party see that Solidarity becomes more stronger, Russians start to fear.'

'They began to see blues under the bed?' Keith suggested. He found to his surprise that the glass which he had been cautiously emptying was full again.

'Is right,' Butch said. 'How you know we say that? Is not good translation, but near. So. General Jaruzelski is Prime Minister and leader of Polish Communist Party, both. Behind him is Polish army. Behind Polish army is Russian army. Military council is formed and they make ...' She snapped her fingers.

'Martial law,' said a voice.

'Is right. They make show of talking to Lech Walesa and other Solidarity leaders. But mostly is force. Thousands, truly thousands of Solidarity leaders are arrested. They do not say arrested, they say interned. They do not say that Solidarity and right to strike are banned, they say suspended. Is same things. One time, more than fifty thousand were interned. Was terrible time. Was shootings in streets.'

'I thought that things were quieter now,' Keith said.

'On surface, yes. But, deep down, no. The ... the

179

pushing down . . .?'

'Suppression.'

'I thank. The suppressions go on. Guns is still used and Solidarity does not have guns. Solidarity men argue peacefully, and is right to do so. Force is best not used, specially if other man has more force than you. But big troubles will come again some day. When that comes, we not content that Polish army turn guns on unarmed Poles. Communists must see that Solidarity can shoot back.

'But that is only beginning,' Butch said. She was picking her way slowly through the still unfamiliar language. 'First we need guns in littler numbers for local troubles. There will be disasters, but world will see that we do not lie down to Russians.

'Poles do not want to be second-class Russians, want to be free. But how to do this? We can not, what you say, vote with feet. Can not vote at all. Freedom can only be bought with blood. Some day comes the big fight. That day we want guns for every Solidarity man, and all those who think the same, if they are ready to fight. Then maybe Polish army will see who are their brothers.'

Butch spoke on in her Anglo-Scots and sometimes falling back on Polish. The room warmed to her words. Drinks were circulating, but no glass went to a mouth without being raised to her first in a silent toast. Keith sensed that he had been admitted to the circle. He was on his third, or possibly fourth, of what he now found to be a mild and palatable drink. It was dawning on him that he had there the client of his dreams, with treasures to sell and an enormous need for firearms. In the cold light of sobriety the proposition would have been too large for comfort. Indeed, cold feet would no doubt make their customary appearance in the morning. But tonight was his night for dealing. Solidarity, he had read somewhere, already had ten million members ....

Butch brought her peroration to a close in a roar of applause. When it had died down she resumed her explanation. 'Before I come to London, it is known to a few friends that I wish to defect. Man comes to speak with me. I am told plan. Ship-people have already promised help. Now agents are wanted in free countries, Britain in special. Polish treasures, all hidden from Russians, is smuggled out to buy guns which is smuggled back and stored until day when is needed. Old guns is not only treasures, is stamps, jewels, gold, pictures and books, maybe other things. But I am to sell guns and to find way to buy new guns.'

'With all that money coming,' Keith said, 'you can buy all the guns you need. Why did you take the risk of hijacking them? It could have blow your whole operation.'

'Just so we think also,' Butch said. 'But we think is first troubles coming soon. And is not easy buying new guns. Is permits and licences and certificates wanted. There are big dealers, international dealers, who are above these things, but these are not in your yellow pages. So how we find? Go to Polish Embassy? Or ask too many questions and so tell Russians what we do? On black market can buy one here and two there, all different size bullets. We thinking maybe you can help. While we think, we get chance to take. Maybe impetuous, you right. But we felt big need. Is not to save the money. We want to pay. Feel bad, not paying. But who we pay now, Eddie Adoni? He is in the jile.'

Keith opened his mouth and closed it again.

'I have the better idea,' Butch said. 'Where my bag?' Her leather bag was passed from table to table until it reached her. She took out a bundle of tissue paper and unwrapped the Russian miquelet pistol. It was even more beautiful than when Keith had last seen it.

'Taking those guns and paying nothing, that makes me feel bad, like thief,' Butch said. 'Is not good to start our dealings like that. This pistol is not such value as the guns we took but, OK, so we get bargain. In business is all right to get bargain, but to take and give nothing is bad. So what I do, I give you this pistol and you promise to hold your wheesht and to help us buy more guns.'

'On the same commission?' Keith asked.

'On same commission. Is deal?'

'Is deal,' Keith said.

They shook hands. There was a murmur of approval. 'You have drink,' Butch said.

Jan Batory, his grim face almost smiling, pushed a larger glass into Keith's hand. 'Stirrup cup,' he said. 'One for the road.'

'He means wee doch-an-dorris,' Butch translated.

Keith had a feeling that he was expected to down the drink in one gulp and then to dash the glass into the fireplace if there were one. Instinct warned him that he had had enough. It usually did, but too late. He sipped at the drink while he thought about the snags ahead. Suddenly the contents of his glass had vanished. He lurched to his feet. Butch came out onto the silent landing with him.

'I'll not be able to put the purchase of hundreds of new firearms through the firm's books,' Keith said. 'So this is a personal deal between you and me. Yes?'

She nodded happily.

'And no cheques,' he added.

She understood him immediately. 'All cash,' she said. 'Or, if you want, I make you present of old guns to value

182

of your commissions?'

'Just what I was thinking myself,' Keith said. He beamed at her. Already he could see the magnificent additions to his personal collection; additions which Wallace could not possibly argue should be part of the firm's stock.

But Butch had not accompanied him in order to discuss business. 'Does Ronnee know that I use what he told me so we can steal guns?' she asked.

With an effort, Keith brought her into focus. She no longer looked like a leader nor even a ballerina. She was just a girl.

'He's worried,' Keith said. 'I think that he's trying not to think about it because he doesn't want to work it out for himself. Why don't you go to him and explain?'

She shook her head violently. 'Is secret. And you promise not to tell.'

'Then just go and smile at him. He'll roll over to have his tummy tickled. You'll see.'

'Not yet,' she said sadly. 'I am ashamed. I break his trust. If he hate me now, I think I die.'

The glow which pervaded Keith's being attained a new level. It was not often given to him to play Cupid. 'Come to us for a drink and a meal tomorrow evening,' he said. 'We can settle some more of the details.'

He managed not to stumble on the stairs. The evening air helped to clear his mind but it turned his knees to rubber. If he had been asked to inflate a breathalyser he suspected that the little plastic bag would dissolve. He left his car where it was and walked down to the hotel. He stopped once and took out the miquelet pistol to gloat over it. Even under the light of a street-lamp in the deepening dusk, it glowed.

FIFTEEN

The Polish Club was not the only centre of conviviality. Younger members of Newton Lauder's population, who had been known to refer to the town's principal hotel as a joint, would have been justified that evening in describing it as jumping. Even in the entrance hall, Keith was aware of the drone of many voices and the sound of laughter.

Mrs Enterkin was behind the reception desk, a duty which she sometimes undertook in times of stress. 'What's going on?' he asked her. 'Not Burns Night?'

'It's the wrong end of the year for that,' she said, laughing. 'What have you been drinking? No, there's no function on. But with the action over and no more news expected until tomorrow, the reporters have got a party going in the big bar. I suppose they're all buying each other drinks on their expense accounts. And there's another party in the lounge, mostly of the men we thought were agents. But they seem to get on very well together,' she added doubtfully.

'I'm told that they usually do, when circumstances allow.' The penultimate word gave Keith a little difficulty. 'Is anybody using the small parlour?'

'Not at the moment, my dear. The locals have all

moved into the public where they can be unsociable together.'

'I'll use the parlour then. Would you dig Mr Smithers out of the cocktail bar and ask him to join me? And don't shout it out.'

'The black man?'

'Is he black?' Keith should have guessed it from the deep, rich voice. But somehow he had not associated the name Smithers and an Oxford accent with colour. He began to wonder what bricks he might have dropped.

'As the ace of spades, my dear,' Mrs Enterkin said. 'You go on through. I'll whisper in his ear.'

'He'll enjoy that,' Keith said. 'I would.' He moved through into the small parlour and concentrated on blowing the mists of alcohol off the surface of his mind.

Mr Smithers, when he arrived, was accompanied by a waiter bearing two glasses and an ice-bucket containing a bottle of champagne. The waiter accepted a tip which seemed to gratify him and withdrew. Keith and Mr Smithers shook hands and sat down.

'You'll join me?' Mr Smithers asked. He was a handsome and well-built negro of early middle-age. His hair was smartly trimmed and his nails manicured to perfection. These might only have been the gloss which the service at Millmont House was liable to impress on its customers, but even Keith, himself the least clothes-conscious of men, realised that the suit and shoes must together have cost the value of a medium-priced shotgun.

'I don't think I should but I probably will,' Keith said. 'Do you have a car with you?'

'One of the Millmont House cars, with driver.'

'Then I'll join you,' Keith said. 'Perhaps you'll be good enough to drop me at my home on your way back.

If all else fails, just pour me through the letter-box.'

Mr Smithers looked concerned. 'What have you been drinking?' he asked.

'I wish I knew.'

'One of those evenings? From what I've been able to learn during the day, you had good cause for celebration; so you may as well continue. I'll see that you reach home safely.' He poured champagne.

'You're enjoying your stay at Millmont House?' Keith enquired.

Mr Smithers smiled, showing very white and even teeth. They had not, Keith noticed, been filed. 'Enormously,' he said. 'Everything is quite delightful. I shall be sorry when our business is concluded and I must leave. His Excellency is not a devotee of the fleshpots and I shall miss my comforts. For the moment, you understand, I am on an expense account. Generous as His Excellency is in the matter of salary, it would hardly keep me in the manner to which Millmont House is accustoming me. Tell me, have you seen any trace of the guns which are still missing?'

Keith put down his glass. The chilled wine was delicious but it seemed tame after the concoction of the Polish Club. 'I'm afraid not,' he said. 'I have a hunch that those guns are gone beyond recall.'

'That is unfortunate,' Mr Smithers said, his cheerfulness undiminished. 'But they were well insured. Which reminds me. I am assured by Superintendent Munro that you were not only responsible for locating the load of guns but also led what one might call the relief expedition. His Excellency is pleased and so are his insurers. In time, the reward will be paid.'

'I'm pleased to hear it,' Keith said. 'And would you like me to find replacements for those that went missing?'

186

'I was going to ask you to do so, once we are sure that they will not be recovered.'

'That also may take some time,' Keith said, feeling his way.

'I think that I can reconcile His Excellency to a certain delay,' Mr Smithers said. Keith understood that an extension of his time at Millmont House would cause Mr Smithers little or no distress.

'You had better let me have copies of your licences to purchase,' Keith said. 'And a note stating that I'm empowered to act for His Excellency. Er – do the papers contain any limitation as to numbers?'

Mr Smithers raised his eyebrows. 'None at all. The more we buy, the happier your government will be. Why do you ask?'

'Because,' Keith said, 'I might be able to put you in the way of affording some extra time at Millmont House on your own account. Would that interest you?'

'Few things would interest me more,' Mr Smithers said earnestly. 'Provided, of course, that it did not involve me in anything contrary to His Excellency's interests.'

'I seem to remember that he's anti-communist,' Keith said.

'Nothing makes him see red except red.'

'Then we can deal. I have another customer. He wants to export a large number of guns. They would not be going in your direction,' Keith explained carefully. 'If they were going, for instance, to the Afghanistan rebels, I take it that His Excellency would approve?'

'Without a doubt.'

'There's no trouble about shipping,' Keith said, 'but he is having difficulty making his purchases. For a small commission, would you care to place the orders and

187

make the payments?'

Mr Smithers nodded thoughtfully and poured more champagne. 'How small a commission?' he enquired.

'A small percentage but on large numbers. All you'd have to do would be to sign a few letters and make some phone-calls at my dictation.'

'We can work out something along those lines,' Mr Smithers said. 'Did the un-numbered, stainless steel Browning turn up? Or has it gone beyond recall?'

'It turned up,' Keith said.

'His Excellency will be pleased. He is particularly anxious to have it for his personal use. And he was delighted with your idea for the engraving.'

'He was?' The champagne was getting to Keith. If he had made a suggestion, he had forgotten it.

'He was indeed. Two missionaries boiling a cannibal. Very topical in view of the present conflict between His Excellency and the established church. It will make an excellent conversation-piece. Perhaps you could put it in hand?'

'Certainly.' Keith held out his glass for a refill. The artistic perfection of a large deal in which he could earn a commission without ever taking overt action was worth celebrating. 'Your English is very good,' he said.

Mr Smithers laughed. 'Fettes College and St Andrews University,' he said. 'I can drop into a good Scots accent when I need it.'

'That's good,' Keith said. 'You may need it soon.'

SIXTEEN

Molly has never given up. To this day she will occasionally demand that Keith tell her what were the three little words which she spoke and which gave him the clue he needed.

But Keith evades the question. He does not feel inclined to tell her that the words which so timeously reminded him of her brother's foreign connection were 'Up the pole'.